In His Time

Stefanie Bridges-Mikota

Edited by Grace Augustine

Cover design by Tell ~ Tale Book Covers

Author Photo by Heidi Marshall Photograpy

Stefanie Bridges-Mikota

In His Time

This book is a work of fiction. While the events regarding the typhoid epidemic are true, most of the characters are a work of the author's imagination. A few mentions of notable true people are used when appropriately necessary to keep the historical information as accurate as possible. All effort was made to convey the true events factual as much as possible. The author accepts all faults for any errors that may be found.

Stefanie Bridges-Mikota

DEDICATION

To my children:

No matter what life may throw your way, keep your eyes focused above

ACKNOWLEDGMENTS

To my family and friends, I owe a big thank you for all the support showered on me after the release of my first book. Grace and Linda, I again thank you for all the encouragement and support. You both have made me feel like family. Heidi Marshall, thank you for working last minute to clean up last minute errors. I thank my fellow Indie authors who have all assisted me to get this far. Thank you kids for giving up computer time so I could work. And for staying quiet, most of the time. Dan, my loving husband, for being patient while I was busy typing away instead of running the house (my regular job), keeping me focused and driven throughout, providing ideas to guide me, and loving me in all the ups and downs during this process. It's the same I said last time, dear, but it still applies.

Coming Soon – For His Will, Book 3
Carried Through Chaos series

by Stefanie Bridges-Mikota

Stefanie Bridges-Mikota

CHAPTER 1

This time Alice Hubbard was excited to ride the train as she headed to her future, not from it. Allie was barely old enough to have a past let alone the one she'd had. She pressed her forehead to the cold window and watched the open land pass by. Her breath fogged up the glass masking the beautiful snowy view of rolling hills and tiny houses with trails of smoke billowing from their chimneys. It appeared a blank slate, a new start. It had been almost a year since she was last on a train. Heading in the other direction, she had fled from her fairytale, turned dangerous life. West was a welcome change of course now.

She knew Frank would be waiting for her at her last stop. He had come ahead of her to make sure that his instincts were right about moving there. His hope was to find a place for them and set it up. Frank had Allie wait until he sent word for her to make the journey.

Allie smiled silently to herself as she thought of the man who was anxiously awaiting her arrival. She had found in Frank a true husband, and gentleman, exactly what her first husband was not. Her smile turned into a scowl at the thought of her first husband and her rosy cheeks paled.

A grey headed lady sat across the aisle from Allie with a hopeful expression on her face. She much reminded Allie of the kind women back home, perhaps those specifically at her church.

"I'm sorry to intrude, but I couldn't help but notice the variety of facial expressions you are making and, well I suppose I'm being nosy, but can I ask what you are thinking about?"

Allie chuckled a little. "Just my past and future is all."

The lady pursed her lips. "You can't be more than just fresh out of school judging by your looks. I can't imagine you really have much of a past."

Honestly, Allie couldn't have imagined it herself had she not lived through it. "Yes, ma'am, indeed I do."

"Well, if you want to talk, seems we both have hours on our hands and no place to be. I'm Doris by the way."

Allie chewed the inside of her cheek a bit while tossing the idea of telling this stranger her history.

Really what could it hurt? Who's she going to tell anyway?

"All right, Doris, seeing as we both have the time. It will help pass part of the trip. My name is Allie. It's nice to meet you, Doris." Doris gave a brief nod and waited expectantly. Allie thought about where to start. There was so much. "Well, to start off, I'm headed to Yakima to meet my husband."

"Oh, you're married? Congratulations! I was married once, long time ago." She looked up at the train's ceiling and sighed.

Allie took that to mean he was most likely no longer part of the living. She didn't want to pry what wasn't offered, though. "Thank you. His name is Frank, and he is wonderful."

Doris started to laugh. "So, you're newly married then?"

Allie was confused. "Yes, how did you know?"

"Well, for starters you are young, although that isn't always as telling as one would hope. But calling your husband wonderful was the other tell-tell sign. You're still in your honeymoon phase."

"Oh," Allie said. If that's where they were, she liked it and didn't want to move on from it. "Well, he is wonderful. He's a doctor. We used to go to school together before he moved to Oregon and became a physician. He worked there for a little while. Then one day we both were riding the same train back to our home town and love planted a seed in our hearts that day. We, of course, didn't know it at the time. I was in a bad way and wasn't thinking all that clearly but looking back it was then that started us on the path we find ourselves on here today."

Doris tucked the "Bad way" information as she called it back and wanted to hear more of the good. "Tell me about your wedding, dear."

Allie closed her eyes deep in thought.

"It was just after Thanksgiving. I initially thought I

wanted to wait a bit before jumping back in, but in my heart, I knew where I belonged. I'd been sweet on Frank for years before he ever took notice in me. Once he finally did set his eyes on mine, I was already bound to someone else. But that's getting off subject. Our wedding was in our home church with both our families and all our friends watching on. It was a simple affair, although Frank's mother would not let me wear something I already had. She paid for a dress to be made for me instead. The dress, my dress, was cream in color. A lacy fabric crossed over the bodice here," she used her hands to show how it laid. "And pulled in at the waist tied with a satin bow. The bottom had a lacy ruffle that just swept the floor in the front and trailed slightly behind me in the back. Oh, I felt like a princess wearing it. I, of course, didn't want Frank's parents to spend that money, but they insisted. They own the bank back home. They are fine folks."

Doris listened with rapt attention. "The wedding sounds lovely. I am curious though, you said you were bound to another? Were you promised to someone else?"

Allie looked down at her hands. "No. I was already married."

Doris gasped. "No. What happened?"

Allie smoothed her up-swept hair and squirmed a bit, "Well, I... see, uh... my first husband was a con. Eddie was charming and friendly at first, but after a short time turned he became abusive and controlling." She wished it wasn't hard to talk about anymore. She still felt shame and the blows landed on her daily.

Doris' stomach sank, and her wrinkled brow furrowed.

She reached a hand to Allie's shoulder in comfort. "I'm very sorry to hear that. What happened to Eddie though? Did you divorce?"

"I was planning on it. I didn't have to."

"I don't understand then. How are you married to another now?" Doris was very confused.

"I ran. Eddie tried to follow and found new work for a time. He ended up fighting the wildfire and the fire won."

Doris was aghast and didn't know what to say to Allie. She knew from personal experience what a traumatic time it must have been. A subject change was needed to pull them both out of the depression they were working towards.

"Tell me about where you are going."

"Wiley City," she instantly picked up her mood. "It's just south of North Yakima. Frank is there now waiting for me. He went ahead first to find a home and prepare it for us. He's been writing to me and teaching me about life there and the area's history as he learns it. I find it so fascinating!"

Doris was pleased the conversation turned for the better. "What parts fascinated you?"

"Well, Wiley City is just being formed and there are other little towns that circle the main city. That's North Yakima." Doris nodded to say she was following. "The medical need is there for white man, but also for the natives that are converting or just desperate for help. North Yakima itself is being served, but those small towns need someone who can travel around and see to people in their own homes. Not everyone can or wants to venture to the city. There wasn't a direct call for more doctors, but the area is growing rapidly and that was just what he was looking to jump on."

"It sounds like a wonderful place. Full of life and adventure."

"I'm not so sure I want much adventure after what I've already been though." Allie bit her nail in worry.

"Oh, you're young yet, there is so much more life ahead of you. Just you wait and see."

Allie placed her hands back in her lap and sighed. "Well, I hope the adventure is good then."

"We all hope it's good dear. The reality is everyone has ups and downs, though. Let's hope you are on the uphill side of this down you recently found yourself in, but life isn't always kind to everyone. For some it seems life kicks them when they are down."

Allie nodded and watched Doris as her eyes seemed to drift to some faraway land. Allie knew her turn for a subject change was here. "Oh, something really fascinating about the town. Did you know when the railroad was being built they approached the town of Yakima City with offers to buy land?"

Doris shook her head no. Her eyes focused back to Allie.

"Yes, and the land owners wanted more than the offer. Do you know what the railroad did?"

Doris again shook her head no.

"They decided to bypass."

"That really doesn't surprise me none. It always comes down to money," Doris tsked.

"They laid their tracks just four miles to the north and then offered free lots to any businesses from Yakima City to relocate. Many took up the offer and moved their existing businesses on roller logs. The first to do so was a hotel. They rolled the four miles in about a months' time, all while having boarders still taking up the rooms and eating in the dining room!"

Allie was still struggling to believe that tale herself. She assumed the hotel must not have been very large.

"Pretty soon the town to the north was called North Yakima and the old Yakima City later, in 1905, changed its name to Union Gap."

"Ladies, would you like your lunch?" A porter came around doling out paper sacks.

They both took theirs and thanked him while giving him coins in return. He nodded and grinned before leaving them back to their conversation.

"Rolled a whole building four miles? That is hard to believe, and I've seen a lot." Doris' eyes were round.

"With people inside, don't forgot that part."

Allie opened her lunch and pulled out an apple. She took a bite and found it to be juicy, but soft.

Doris could tell she didn't really like the apple, "I hear North Yakima is the area where the best apples come from."

"I hope so. This one is mushy." They both chuckled.

They continued their conversation for much of the trip, only stopping long enough to sleep at night. The more they talked the more Allie became comfortable with Doris and the more details she gave. Before too long it seemed, Doris knew much of Allie's history. Doris had shared a bit of hers as well. Allie had made a quick friend and was sad she would have to say goodbye to her soon. Doris would continue on her journey after the train stopped for Allie. She was going over to the Tacoma area to meet up with her family.

Saying goodbye came sooner than Allie had hoped, as North Yakima drew near. She was excited to see Frank and knowing he would be waiting on the walk just as soon as the train stopped lessened the little sting the goodbye would bring.

CHAPTER 2

Frank was standing tall on the boardwalk aside the track as the train rolled to a stop. Allie giggled as Frank lent her his hand off the train and wisped her up in his arms.

"Welcome to Washington my dear," Frank said as he set her down gently.

"Thank you fine sir." Allie stretched a bit. "It feels good to be off the train." She scanned the area while Frank fetched her bags.

Allie was shocked to see North Yakima upon her arrival. It was still relatively small, but a very busy place. The streets were lined with trees, and ditches had been dug along the streets to carry water for irrigation.

The stench was horrendous, as there were dairy farms close by and in town. Streets were pocked with horse manure, rotting food, and other filth. She was glad to know that she wouldn't be living there. They were headed a short distance to the southwest of the city.

Wiley City was small compared to Deer Lodge, but it was also younger and thus had less time to grow. Allie took in the sites as she sat in the open wagon next to Frank. A Morgan horse named Penny was pulling them along at a steady clip.

It was a bitter day and there was a dusting of snow on the ground, but Frank brought a blanket along for her to wrap up in to keep warm. He was always very thoughtful. Frank was driving her home. The word home brought a sense of warmth that filled her chest and left her tingling with excitement.

Allie was accustomed to hills and mountains covered with trees. The first stretch of her trip west showed the scarring of the fire that decimated areas so few months before. Here the hills looked scalped, but it was not from fire. The land wasn't completely barren. Trees dotted the landscape here and there on the flats where the town lay, but the hills that surrounded them looked like someone took a straight edge and shaved them clean. The lack of vegetation meant she could see much farther than where she lived with her first husband.

Falcon, Idaho was crammed with trees. It made one feel closed in. This area looked similar to her home town, although her hills had many trees. The flats were similar enough that they made her feel at ease with her future.

It was easy to spot the streams and creeks as they had the most vegetation lining their banks. Allie hoped her home had a creek nearby. Flowing water washing over her was balm to her soul on a warm afternoon.

As they drove down the main street Allie noticed all of the structures were built out of wood. She wondered just how far away that wood must have been shipped to get here. Frank had told her that farther west was a mountain pass separating the East from the West. She assumed the trees must have come from that direction.

The town was primitive compared to her home town. Roads were dirt and there were no formal foot paths or boardwalks. Many of the buildings had a western theme.

Frank pulled the wagon up to a small two-story wood house that fronted Hughes Road. It wasn't the main street through town, but a side road that shot off of it. In all her life she had never lived in town and was glad that at least they wouldn't be right in the middle of the main business area.

The house was plain, but hopeful with possibilities. The building was in good condition since it was newly built. The yard was nothing to speak of and she knew right away she wanted a little picket fence in front. She could envision a wooden swing hanging from the tree on the side, awaiting the play of children. Someday, rocking chairs on the front porch overlooking the road would be nice.

Frank jumped down and walked around to help her out of the rig.

"Welcome home darling," he whispered as he kissed her cheek.

Frank took her hand and walked to the door of the house. His eyes twinkled with enthusiasm as he opened the door and let her in first.

"Now, I know it's nothing much yet, but it's in a good location and there's a side door that with a little tweaking could be used as my practice entrance."

"It's wonderful, Frank," Allie said with a wide grin. She turned in a circle and took in the small foyer that opened to the front room. Silently she was taking it all in and then stopped.

"Where do the horse and wagon go? I didn't see a barn outside."

"There isn't one. I board them at the livery stable owned also by the Wiley's just a short distance from here. Someday maybe we will buy our own land and build our house with a barn. For now, though, this will do." Frank grabbed her hand, "Come on, I'll give you the tour."

He walked her through the living room that had a fireplace on the outer wall and held two padded chairs with a side table between. They walked into the dining room and Frank pointed out the side door that exited from this room. From there they turned to the kitchen, complete with a stove, sink with a hand pump, and counter.

Stairs flanked the wall that supported the middle of the house. Just behind the stairs and off the kitchen was a small bath. Upstairs there were three bedrooms, one of which had a bed. The others lay empty, awaiting a future tenant.

Maybe one day those rooms will be full, Allie thought, but refused to give voice to the notion.

Frank hurried her back down stairs and into the front room. He motioned for her to sit.

"Now I know this is sparsely decorated. I hope you can make quick work on that end..."

"Of course, I can," Allie interrupted. "I made curtains

with the dimensions you gave me and a quilt for the bed while I was waiting to come out. Ma also shared what she could - some towels, a set of sheets, and some odds and ends for the kitchen. We also have the wedding gifts that you hadn't already brought with you. They're all in the trunk out in the wagon. We need more furniture, but I'm sure we can get by with what is here for a while."

Frank smiled and thought she was being so positive. Seeing the bright side to matters like this came naturally to her.

"I'm sure you will. As for my practice, I thought we could build a wall to partition off the dining room since the side door could be easily used for business only. That would leave a hallway connecting the living room and kitchen. It would also be convenient for me to clean up in between patients. Dr. Leman always stressed cleanliness to me. I'm so glad he did."

Allie folded her hands waiting for Frank to continue. She could tell he was turning the conversation into a serious topic and became a bit on edge for what was to come.

"Typhoid seems to be a growing issue here. I know you saw the filth in Yakima. I have met with the other doctors and together we are working to educate the population to clean things up. Many people are turning a deaf ear to us, though. They don't see it as a problem. I will continue to keep working to make this a safer place for all, but in the meantime, I need a few things from you."

Frank looked at Allie to make sure she was completely following and understanding the severity of the issue before continuing.

"You probably took note of the pump and sink in the kitchen. I need you to boil any and all water you use even from the pump. Cooking, cleaning, washing up - it all needs to be boiled first before using. We have our own well and that should be fine, but until we know for certain where the disease is coming from and how it's spreading, we must stay vigilant."

Allie was speechless, shocked into silence. She stood and walked to the window. Staring out, she could see the closest creek. "Does that also mean swimming is out of the cards?"

Frank knew the relationship Allie had with water. "I think if you don't drink it and you wash up after, you will be fine. That water isn't stagnant and the creeks close by run to the Yakima River. The Yakima runs right through the city. These tributaries should be cleaner due to just being away from that mess. You might need to get permission from the Wiley family first, though, it's not on this lot. That family homesteaded the area and own most of the land this town sits on"

"Have you met them? Are they nice folks?" Allie was eager to learn more about her new home.

Frank stood and walked over to the window standing next to Allie. He put his hands on Allie's shoulders, turning her toward him.

"They are wonderful people. Very hard working good folks. The street we are living on was actually named after the senior Wiley – Mr. Hugh Wiley. He was the first settler to this area. Allie, I know this is both exciting and terrifying for you. Starting a-new is full of hope and worry of what is to come. You have been through much in the last couple of years. I'm here.

Lean on me. Let me be your rock. We will build a life here and thrive. This future will be much better than your last."

Allie drew in a deep breath as she locked eyes with her husband. He had the deepest chocolate-colored eyes. She knew she could trust this man with her life, but knowing that and feeling it was a different matter.

She knew Eddie was dead and could no longer hurt her. It didn't mean she didn't still feel vulnerable, though. She still startled easily. She wondered if she did something that it would upset Frank the way Eddie got upset. Frank had never shown a temper directed towards anyone. Sure, he'd gotten angry at times, but he never harmed anyone.

Working to remove those thoughts would take time, but Allie hoped one day she could get to that place - the place where she could fully relax in all situations. She leaned in and kissed her husband for the first time in their new home.

CHAPTER 3

March was right around the corner and although Allie was settling in nicely, she missed her community and hoped she'd form some deep friendships soon.

Frank had hung her bright yellow curtains in their bedroom. Her Ma had some in hers and they always put her in a more cheerful mood. The quilt was laid on the bed. It was a simple quilt with squares of alternating fabric, a yellow floral print and the other was a solid navy.

The downstairs room's windows were covered with plain brown curtains. She wanted to keep the downstairs fairly neutral since she wasn't sure how the medical practice would tie into the floorplan.

The living room chairs had wood legs and arms with a red floral pattern on the seat and back. She would love a davenport someday, but first she knew they needed a kitchen table and chairs. Since the dining room was to be converted, they would place a table in the middle of the kitchen and eat there. There was enough kitchen-ware to get them started:

towels, rags, a rolling pin, two cast iron pans and one pot, a few cooking utensils, plus a couple of dishes with silverware and glasses. Between her Ma and the church ladies, they set them up fairly well in the kitchen department.

Frank was already working on the plans for the renovation. Because they were renting from the Wiley family, he needed their permission before starting. Frank would bring a much-needed service to this area and the Wiley's had no issues with his idea. They even offered to chip in and asked the other town folk to help with the materials and labor.

That was good news for Frank as he never did learn much about building. His father made sure to teach him all about banking and his Ma believed a man should know basic life skills such as cooking and mending but learning about carpentry was an opportunity that never presented itself.

Frank was eager to get his hands on the wood and learn something from these people, though. With the proposed layout, one wall shortening the room would allow a hallway between the living and kitchen, and that was all that was needed. They all thought it could be put up in a few days' time. That was good news for Frank, too. He needed to start actually practicing medicine, so he wouldn't have to live off his savings.

A group of four men came on a Tuesday with a wagon full of lumber. Frank introduced them as brothers, John and Bill Wiley, Peter Baxter, and Richard North. Those men moved fast, too. That didn't really surprise Allie any, though. Her Pa was very handy with his hands and could also work quickly.

In one day they had the wall framed with a spot for a door Frank could use so he didn't have to go outside to go between home and work. Also, he could wash his instruments between patients quicker with having easy access to the kitchen sink. Allie just needed to remember to keep boiled water handy at all times for him.

The next day started the next phase. They called it lath and plaster. Allie didn't know what that was, and she wasn't really interested in finding out. Building a wall was boring and noisy. She mostly just stayed out of their way, hiding out in their bedroom writing letters to her Ma and Blinne and several others.

Blinne had been her best friend since they were young children. They parted when Allie left town with her first husband. Blinne married another childhood friend named George and moved into his grandparent's old home. They had one daughter, Lena, and another one on the way. That pregnancy was still fairly early. She had discovered she was with child just before Allie and Frank wed.

Allie missed Blinne dearly. They told each other everything and helped each other through difficult times. It would be hard to find someone to take her place and she wasn't really sure she wanted anyone to do that. No one can really know you unless they grow with you. Knowing someone's present makes fine friendships, but knowing their past brings a deeper level of understanding of the person. Sharing much of that past makes them family.

With her letters written, she walked downstairs to check the renovation progress. Frank was right in the middle of things and covered up to his elbows in plaster. He was smearing plaster over the horizontal boards pushing it between them. He didn't notice her standing there. He was having fun learning something new and she thought that was cute. The other men spotted her and greeted her causing Frank to stop and turn around. Allie started giggling as Frank had plaster on his cheek and in his light brown hair.

"What do you think Allie?" Frank said oblivious to how his face looked.

Through laughter Allie replied, "It looks good... so do you, by the way."

Frank paused and looked down, confused as to what was so funny.

Allie left for the kitchen to get a towel. When she came back she wiped his face off for him in order to keep the towel as clean as possible with his hands not touching it.

Frank smiled and winked at her, realizing why she'd laughed. He turned back to the wall.

"This is the first coat. It will have three by the time we are done. Being just this short wall means it won't take long. Drying between coats will probably take longer than the application of the plaster."

"It sounds like you can start your practice really soon then."

Frank turned back around.

"Yes, but I will need some essentials before then. I did order a few things that will be shipped from back East to

Yakima, but they haven't arrived yet."

"I sure hope they come soon. Going to Yakima to see the doctor isn't awful, but it would sure be nice to have you up and running soon," one of the Wiley brothers stated.

"If you need some help hauling any of that just let me know. I'd be glad to do it," the other Wiley brother added.

"Thanks, that's mighty kind of you."

Frank looked to Allie to see if she was paying attention to the helpfulness of the townspeople. He truly wanted her to feel accepted in this place and by these people like she did back home.

"I wrote some letters. I'd love to post them as soon as possible."

Robert spoke up, "I'm headed there myself in a bit. I'd be happy to post them for you."

"Thank you so much. I'll get them and the post fare for you."

Allie left to retrieve the letters. The men seemed to be well mannered and decent folks, she thought. She sure hoped the women were of the same character. She had met a few already and they seemed nice.

Frank and Allie attended church every Sunday and everyone was friendly, but she hadn't been fully accepted yet. The ladies, she felt, were still feeling her out. When they invited her to join one of their groups, maybe a quilting group, or put her on rotation for the picnics, then she would know they were extending friendship.

Maybe they were waiting on her first or perhaps it just wasn't the busy season, and no one was doing much with the women's groups currently. Her first impressions with the congregation gave her hope. Maybe the ache from missing her parents and closest friends would soon ease a bit as she made new friends. She hoped that came sooner than later.

When she returned downstairs, the men were cleaning up for the day. She was thankful for that. She loved her alone time with her husband and didn't think she could ever grow tired of it. She handed her letters to Robert and thanked him again. The men finished and left for the day. They would be back in the morning to apply another coat.

Frank tried to give her a hug, but she pushed back on him.

"I'll go heat up the water and pour you a bath."

"What? I'm not that dirty," he chuckled and tried again to hug her.

Allie squealed and took off running to the kitchen. Frank smiled and headed outside to try to get at least some of the plaster off before he completely dirtied their tub.

Frank was very hopeful for the future and, so far, things were moving just as planned. He knew that some of the people, many of the natives and a few townsfolk, would not be able to pay up front. He would be taking payments and food and household goods also as payment or part payment for some. A few could pay right away and he would have to rely on those for the time being. He just hoped there were enough people who needed to be seen to get him up and running. Establishing a practice, he thought, would be the harder part. Keeping it going seemed easier. He knew whatever the case may be, he had a great woman supporting him. Together they could achieve anything.

CHAPTER 4

The spring weather was warming. The previous snow had melted and bulbs were poking up out of the ground here and there. Allie couldn't wait to see the flowers in bloom.

Today they were headed to Yakima to pick up what Frank had ordered. Having an exam table was necessary to opening the office, but Frank knew he couldn't load and unload it himself. Robert volunteering to meet them in town was a blessing.

Yakima had an expansive streetcar system and they even had a line that serviced Wiley City. It had opened last June. This meant Allie had a bit more freedom. She could ride the trolley to and from without need of Frank driving or borrowing the rig. She was used to walking everywhere she went, but now with the streetcar, she didn't have to. The walk to the city was a much greater distance than the walk from her farm house to Deer Lodge. Having the city close by and transportation to get her there, but living more in a country location, gave Allie the best of both worlds. She loved that.

Yakima still stunk. She didn't know if she would ever get use to the stench and had hoped that between the first visit and now, improvement would have been made. The smell of cow manure was strong. The roads had droppings scattered here and there from various animals and with garbage randomly thrown, it appeared the city didn't have any sort of system set up yet for this growing need.

Frank dropped off Allie on First Street, so she could do a little shopping in the shops that shared the building with the Pacific Hotel. Frank and Robert headed to pick up the shipments. The hotel was close to the depot where she had first arrived and she recognized a few buildings from before. Some of those buildings housed more shops that she could pass the time in if Frank took a bit longer than expected.

Allie raised her skirt a bit and was careful as to where she placed her feet. She wasn't going to step in any muck between here and the hotel. She entered the building and was greeted by the most wonderful smell. Maybe it was so wonderful just because the outside smell was horrendous. Allie didn't care. She walked into the little bakery and sat at one of the quaint tables. A small rounded lady approached asking if she would like a cup of coffee or tea and something to eat. She ordered tea and a slice of apple pie with sharp cheddar to top it.

"I hope you like it," the woman said. "This pie won a blue ribbon at the fair last year. Well, not this pie, but this recipe," she joked.

"Oh, Yakima has a fair?" Allie was excited having something to look forward to. She and Frank worked in Deer Lodge's fair the previous year.

"Sure do. It's the last Monday in September. We lost the privilege of being state capitol to Olympia, but we have held onto the state fair," the waitress winked and left her to her pie.

As Allie sat enjoying her treat, she watched the busy street through the front window. She thought about what a state fair here would look like. Deer Lodge's fair was the county fair. It was a big deal for them. She was having a hard time imagining what a state fair would look like, let alone how many people would be moving about for it.

Just now, looking out at the street, it seemed people were coming and going in every direction. Horses were thrown in the mix, as well as some dogs, and even a cow or two being pulled on a halter. She guessed since some of the dairy farms were in town, seeing cows in town was not that unusual.

Allie wondered what everyone was doing in their comings and goings. The town was not as well established as she was used to, although it was getting close by the looks of it. It was new. Compared to her hometown, it felt new, albeit dirty. The vegetation had grown up around the buildings there as if they had always been. North Yakima had more people, though. With the last bite of pie in her, she finished her tea, paid the nice woman, and headed out to see what else she might find.

There were several shops in walking distance to choose from. Allie ducked into a furniture store. They had some locally made furniture and some that was shipped into town from various locations. She admired the davenports that were shipped in. They did have a very good selection of locally made tables and chairs. Just a small table with four sturdy legs and two chairs would suit them for now. She hoped one day they would need more chairs, but that possibility was unknown.

Allie had a miscarriage caused from the abuse of her first husband and when Dr. Leman confirmed and had to finish the work that her body tried and failed to do, he told her to be prepared that she may never be able to again carry.

Allie was still trying to come to terms with this possibility. She wasn't sure she could ever be satisfied without carrying her own child and bringing that babe into the world. Life had a way of working itself out in the end and she knew God had a plan and timing for everything. She knew patience would be a test for her. As she wandered through the tables, the bell above the door jingled. She didn't realize it was Frank until he was right beside her.

"Have you found one you like?"

"Oh, my goodness, hi. You startled me." Allie put her hand on her chest to calm her heart.

Frank placed his hand on her back and turned her slightly towards him.

"Sorry dear, didn't mean to scare you. You looked lost in thought. Everything all right?"

Allie took a calming breath before replying that she was fine. She knew Frank was aware of her medical history and the likely difficulties starting a family that laid in front of them. She didn't want to talk about it though.

"I'm just trying to decide if I like one of these table and chair sets. We will eventually need something. Eating in the living room is fine for a while, but I would like to have a real table to sit down and share a meal over."

Frank smirked a bit. "How about we pick one out today? I have room for it in the wagon and I agree, we do need one."

Allie grew a bit excited at that and together they agreed on a basic round table with a single pedestal that had four feet extending from the base. The chairs were round back with spindles all in the color of warm honey. There were more elaborate designed ones with intricate carvings around the edge and even some with inlays, but this one would suite them just fine. Frank paid for it and together, with the shop owner, they loaded it in the wagon and headed for home.

The ride home took a bit longer than coming due to the extra weight and wanting to be careful not to jostle the items. Robert had gone on ahead and would be waiting for them for a short time. The day was beautiful and warmer than it had been since she arrived, but it was still just a bit chilly and she was thankful she had her lap blanket with her.

"Did everything that you were expecting arrive?" Allie turned slightly to Frank.

"It sure did. I can't wait to get it home and start setting up. I picked up some paint and have a nice board I was hoping you would paint a sign for me." Frank raised his brows and looked at her.

Allie's face softened, "I'd love to, and I'll start soon on it."

She loved being useful. When she was barely an adult, not quite a child, she gained her first job waiting tables at a restaurant in town. That's where she was working when she met Eddie. He'd come in to eat and decided before he left he would shortly make Allie his.

Eddie was the perfect gentleman for the first few weeks as he gained Allie's trust and love. He knew precisely what to say to a wide eyed young lady. She learned shortly after marrying him, though, that what she thought she felt wasn't true love.

It took Allie a good while to accept what she knew as true. Once she did, she realized she had to leave to save herself. After escaping back home she found employment working at the local paper. She loved that job and learned much about how to fight for herself.

After the railroad laid off hundreds and her boss let her go to make room for one of those men who needed employment, Frank stood up for her and taught her that she was worthy and just as important, an equal. Now that she was here, she wondered if she was expected to stay home and just do household duties, help with the patients in some way, or if she could find herself something to do. She wasn't yet ready to bring that up to Frank and she would enjoy the little things that she had to do.

They pulled up to the house and Robert had already unloaded the smaller items from his wagon onto the front porch. He walked over and after Frank helped Allie down they worked to get the heavier items out of the back. Allie was the door holder. Once they were in, she worked at moving the smaller packages into the living room for Frank to sort later.

"I'll be back in a bit. Have to go park the steed and carriage," he explained, dropping a kiss on her cheek.

"Oh Frank, stop." Allie swatted at him and shewed him outside. She left the boxes and found some paper and a pencil to begin work on sketching a sign. Perhaps a bold script would stand out, or flowing letters would add some eloquence. Whatever the case, it had to be professional and catch the eye of someone in medical need. She wouldn't start painting until Frank approved it first. It was his business and she wanted him to like it. She wanted him to approve of everything she did and wondered if that would be so if she had never met Eddie. She knew she needed to stop those thoughts, but they seemed to take over every chance they could. Several designs would need to be ready for Frank's review upon his return and she forced her mind back to the present. It was nice to do tasks for him out of love rather than fear.

CHAPTER 5

Frank's practice was up and running, albeit a bit slowly. He was a little frustrated, but knew that this was the most likely way of things and worked to stay patient. There were a few people who came by to see him for very minor issues. One was a black toenail they weren't sure was fungus or not and Frank had determined through questioning the patient that it had been hurt. He explained it would fall off soon and new would regrow, hopefully. There was always a chance that he would forever be missing a toenail, but there was much worse one must deal with than a missing toenail.

A parent brought their child in a with stomach ache that turned out to be just gas. The room had to be aired out for a while after that one. In that moment he was thankful that they built a full wall with a door, so the rest of the house didn't suffer as well.

There was a woman who had some basic pregnancy symptoms and Frank was happy to confirm the news. No Natives came and no one with anything serious yet. It could just be that in this sleepy little town serious medical issues were few and far between.

Frank was used to the revolving door at the Deer Lodge clinic and before that the hustle and bustle of the logging camp in Sandy, Oregon. It would take a bit of adjusting to this schedule. He just hoped he made enough with these minor cases to get by.

Allie always made the most with the little income. That is how she grew up. Her parents are wonderful hard working folks who never complain much. They have just kept pushing forward with what they have. Frank knew that, but he desperately wanted more than that for his wife.

Frank stepped outside to draw in some fresh air and spy if he could see anyone potentially coming. Twiddling his thumbs was becoming a maddening substitute for work. He had rearranged his instruments multiple times. They were polished until they sparkled. The file cabinets were set up and waiting to be filled with patient information. He had a container of lollipops ready for the many children he hoped he would see.

Allie had the household under control and he suspected she was a bit bored as well. Just the two of them didn't cause many messes that required heavy, regular cleaning. Cooking was about the most she had to do and that was mainly because she had to make sure she continually had enough water boiled for not only the meal prep, but also the cleanup.

Frank looked up and saw the sign Allie painted hanging above him. She did a magnificent job on it and one couldn't tell it wasn't professionally done unless they were up close to it. DR. FRANK HUBBARD it read with a fancy curly border. Allie could do anything she put her mind to it had seemed.

Seeing that no one was headed his way, Frank walked back inside to brainstorm. He needed something to do and he knew Allie did, too. An ad in the paper would be one way to go, but he wasn't sure how many Wiley City folks bought the paper from North Yakima.

Wiley City didn't have one of their own. North Yakima townsmen wouldn't travel out here when they had a few doctors to choose from right there. There were other small towns that sat around North Yakima. He wondered if they would have need of an on call doctor. It would mean he would be away from Allie for periods of time and he wasn't sure he was ready to do that... nor was he sure, at this point, how that would even work. He wouldn't have a place to practice there.

With his uncovered wagon it wouldn't be practical to try to run an office from that. The only solution would be to see patients in their own homes. He would be the traveling house call doctor. How to set that up was perplexing to him.

The Catholic Mission was south west of here. They serviced the Natives. Maybe he could be of help there, he thought. Of course, that wouldn't pay, most likely, anything. It would be something to do to pass the time, though. Gaining the trust of the Natives could also be beneficial in the long run.

He stepped into the hall and listened to see if he could hear where Allie was. Downstairs was silent, so he treaded the stairs to find her in their room writing a letter. "Hey Allie."

She held up her finger indicating to give her a moment to finish her thought. She was sitting at the little desk writing what Frank thought most likely was a letter. After she finished, she turned and smiled at her husband.

"He walked over to her and gave her a kiss before taking a seat on the bed. "I've been thinking…"

"Uh Oh!" Allie teased trying to lighten the air that seemed to hang around him.

"I'm serious right now," Frank stated with furrowed brows, making Allie's hazel eyes widen just a bit.

"You know I haven't had many patients yet, and I'm trying to find a way to boost business, or at least give me something to do to pass the time."

"Well you just started a couple of weeks ago. I would think this would take some time, don't you?" Allie stood and moved slightly away as in habit.

Frank realized the significance of her actions and immediately changed his tone.

"Yes, of course, but I'm bored. I need something more to do."

He laid back on the bed with his arms and legs spread and gazed at the ceiling. Allie remained where she stood, but relaxed her posture realizing that Frank wasn't angry.

"I figure I have two options, or I could do both. First is to travel to the other local towns and see if there is a need. If I find some that do have a need, I could try to set up a day every week or every couple of weeks to go regularly to see patients in their homes. The other option is to head to the mission and try to serve the needs of the Natives," he explained and sat back up, watching Allie as she processed the options.

Allie chewed on these a bit as she paced the room. Helping the Natives would be a kind gesture and it might even earn some trust from the locals, but she knew it wouldn't bring in income. The surrounding towns would require him to be gone longer than just a day. She went round and round for a bit before she spoke.

"What if you start with the towns and see just what kind of need there might be? Maybe there isn't any or maybe that will keep you busy most of the time. Then, if time allows, you can head to the mission and work in-between your rounds? I'm thinking keeping your practice open here three to four days a week and work the small towns one or two days with the mission taking a day once a month."

Frank stood and walked to her. "I like it. It's the best of both. I'll make some arrangements and head out early next week to see what I can drum up."

"Maybe I can go with you and help with getting started and then keeping files organized and setting up appointments?" Allie was hopeful, but didn't want to fall too hard if he said no.

Frank wrapped his arms around her and whispered in her ear, "That sounds like a great idea. I love you sweetheart."

Allie melted in his arms and excitement for her new challenge lifted her spirit higher. Finally, a man that appreciated her for her brains and beauty. Frank chuckled and pulled her down on the bed with him. This time, Allie gave in without hesitation to his warm embrace.

CHAPTER 6

Frank and Allie set out first to Ahtanum. The town was only two miles east from Wiley City, making it an easy day trip and they would even make it home well before dark. It was conceivable that the folks from there might go to Wiley City to see him instead of into Yakima. After that trip they would need to take several days to head to Parker, Tampico, and the surrounding area.

Allie had made little cards that matched the sign above the office and on the back gave their address. They were to be handed door to door to help spread the word about the new doctor. Whether that was good advertising or not was yet to be seen.

The trip was pleasant. They stopped at many of the houses they came across and most greeted them warmly. A few welcomed them in for a cup of coffee, which was nice on this still cool day.

Of course, anyone could go to Yakima and see Dr. Green, or they could head south to Dr. Harvey or Dr. Campbell.

Frank was just one more choice for them. Time would tell if this trip would pick up traffic at his office. Being so close, he didn't see a need to set up a particular day each week to go see them. They could always do that later if it seemed there was a big enough need.

On the way home they stopped by a field and ate a picnic lunch Allie had packed. It was a bit later than lunch time and their stomachs let them know that fact. They didn't want to stop in the middle of meeting the people, so they pressed on until they were ready to head for home.

Once they reached Wiley City, Allie asked Frank to stop at the post before turning for home. There was plenty of time before dark so he obliged. She was waiting for letters to arrive from Deer Lodge. She had sent a few already. Finding things to do to fill her days was tough so she had a lot of writing time on her hands. She needed something to do. If she had children that would most certainly occupy her time and she would be overjoyed. Somehow she had to come to terms with the likelihood of that not panning out. Something that she could do away from home would help. She wasn't sure where she would be needed and wanted, though.

Frank parked the wagon and Allie went in to retrieve the mail. When she returned she had an excited smile on her face.

"Two! I have two, one from Ma and the other from Blinne." Allie climbed up and sat atop her lap blanket. She was paying little attention to the cool air now.

"I'll drive you read. Out loud if you don't mind, but if you'd rather keep them private that is fine, too." Frank took the reins and once again they were headed for home.

Allie opened Blinne's first. She scanned the letter before deciding she could read it out loud.

Hello,

It was wonderful to hear from you. I am so glad to know that you arrived safe and have settled in well. Honestly, I was worried about you. You are fearless! I have never been away from Deer Lodge let alone by myself. I can't imagine how I would do on a train traveling so far away alone.

Lena is growing like a weed. She is already eight months old and is crawling all over. It's hard to keep up with her at times. This pregnancy has me very tired and I am still sick at times. Doc says I'm somewhere around three months along. This babe should arrive around September. I'm not sure what I will do with two kids, one just born and another just a bit over one. Life is going to get busy very quickly.

Allie paused absorbing that and found her heart to be a bit bitter about it. She wanted to be happy for Blinne, but was struggling to see it that way. What she wouldn't give to trade places with Blinne, but then she looked over and realized that would mean she wouldn't have Frank either. She shook her head a bit and continued to read.

George is doing well. He is so proud he walks around with his chest puffed out. Lena is his little girl and she already knows it. That stinker will cry and cry for me, but as soon as daddy gets home she is all smiles for him. I just can't compete with her cuteness and I won't even try. She steals the hearts of all the men she is around. We will need to watch that one when she gets older.

I better get going. I only have so much time during nap time to get much done. I hope this letter finds you well and look forward to hearing from you again.

Blinne

Allie folded the letter and put it back in its envelope.

"I'm happy for them aren't you?" Frank tipped his head to the side to look at her.

Allie lowered her eyes to her hands that were folded in her lap on top of the letters…

"I am. I'm so glad she found her happily ever after. She seems to be loving her life."

Frank put his hand on hers and squeezed a bit. Allie looked up and gave a small sad smile. They both knew her hopes for children and fears that it wouldn't be possible, but neither voiced them.

"On to the next one, if you still want to read out loud."

Allie opened the letter from her Ma and scanned it. She furrowed her brows. "This doesn't sound good Frank." Allie kept reading silently.

"What do you mean? Read it out loud please?"

My Dear Sweet Allie Girl,

Thank you for the letter. I love hearing from you and miss you so much already. You bring a joy to this house that goes missing

38

when you leave. Drew misses you the most. He retreated to his room for a while, but has since started doing more again. It takes him a while to process change. Pa is hard as nails and just goes on like nothing has changed. I find my days quiet. I miss having you around to talk to. Being the only female in the house again makes for a lonely time.

Here in the last couple of weeks I have developed a cough and have a bump in the middle of my throat. Doc Leman is sure I just have a virus, so plenty of rest for me. You know how well I rest. At least it isn't watering season.

Allie paused and looked to Frank. "What do you think that means? Does she just have a cold?"

Frank hesitated as he thought about the symptoms.

"I'm sure Doc is right. He's a good doctor and I wouldn't second guess him. The bump she talks about is probably just a swollen lymph gland. We have them all over our bodies. Sometimes when we get sick they get swollen. If she can follow orders, I'm sure she will recover quickly." Frank wasn't sure he came across very convincing, certainly not to himself. He began chewing on the inside of his cheek and contemplated the other possible condition she could have, but wouldn't worry Allie right now. "Go on. Does she say more?"

Last year with the worst drought in

history, watering was awful. I would love not to see another year like that in my lifetime. I know I've said this already to you, but your timing in coming home was a Godsend. I know why you came home, but God made that work for the good for many people. Thank you for being brave and strong to do that. I know you were scared, but you kept a brave face and kept on despite the fear. I will always be proud of you.

I hope you and Frank are enjoying married life. The newlywed time can be a time of much fun and also lots of learning and growth for the relationship. Please keep God at your center and rely on him. A foundation built on Him will never fail. I love you, sweet Allie, and will write again soon. I need to go back and rest like Doc said.

Love

Always,

Ma

"I really hope you are right, that she will be fine. I have a bad feeling about this."

Allie folded up the second letter and returned it to its envelope. Placing the letters in her lap she worried her thumb on her index finger.

"I'm sure it will be. Let me know when she writes again. I want to follow and make sure she is fine."

Frank directed the horse to the livery stables. They were within walking distance to home and the weather was perfect for a stroll with his wife. He hoped that might help take her mind off the letters.

CHAPTER 7

The following week Frank had a bit more traffic to the office. That pleased him. It turned out that leaving those cards Allie had made was working. Word had been spreading into the city that there was a new doctor in town. He wasn't sure if he would need to head to the other outlying communities now or not. Time would tell, but for now he would stay put and see to his new patients.

As the week wore on, Frank couldn't get the letter from Allie's Ma out of his head. He knew Doc Leman was a great doctor, but was struggling to believe Ma's condition was a simple common virus. He decided to write Doc himself and see if he could glean any more information from him.

He wanted to catch Doc up on the goings on here, too, anyway. He would also be waiting to hear anything more from Ma. Allie hadn't been gone that long yet. She had said that everything seemed fine when she was there. Ma was still just as feisty and busy as ever. For Ma to seek out Doc Leman's help something was definitely up. He just wasn't ready to say aloud what he thought she might be suffering from.

Frank worked to clean up his instruments and get them back in place before he wrote his letter, so all would be ready when the next visitor arrived. Visitor... that was all some of his patients really were. Some folks just wanted to see who the new people were in town even if they had to pay for his service to do it. He really wasn't sure why they just didn't knock on the front door instead. There they could make introductions like regular folk and it would be free. Oh well, business was up and that was all he needed for now.

He had sat down and was part way through writing his letter when another person arrived at the door. He welcomed her in and asked her to sit.

"Good afternoon, Ma'am. My name is Doctor Hubbard. What can I do for you today?"

"Hello, doctor. I'm Mrs. Geoffrey. Isabelle Geoffrey. I don't have an issue needing attention just now, but I did want to drop by and say my hellos and offer to host you and your wife to dinner this Friday night. I really should have been here sooner," she wet her lips and paused. "I've seen you at church a few times now, this area sure is growing mighty fast. We get used to our circles and then new people show up. We were here before the railroad. Seen a lot of people come this way. Well, look at me just rambling on and on."

Frank shook his head to dispute her last remark. He was interested in the area and wanted to know more. He needed to understand what made this area and these people tick so he knew how to interact with them as their physician.

"Allen and I live just east, outside of town on the left. And don't worry about bringing anything. The two of you will be just fine."

"Well, thank you. That is mighty nice, and my Mrs. will be pleased."

Mrs. Geoffrey stood to leave, so Frank stood and walked her to the door.

"Thank you for stopping by. It was very nice to meet you."

Mrs. Geoffrey nodded.

"Pleased to meet you as well. We will see you Friday around five o'clock." She turned and walked out the door.

Frank was pleased as well. Allie would be tickled. It was their first invite and he knew she needed to make some connections. He decided to leave his letter to Doc Leman unfinished for now and go find Allie. He couldn't wait to share the news with her.

Allie was in the kitchen peeling potatoes for their evening meal. Frank walked up behind her and wrapped his arms around her. She startled at first and then relaxed in his arms.

"You will never guess what just happened?"

Allie sat her knife and potato down on the counter and worked to turn in his arms.

"Well let me see," she took her finger and tapped her chin. "You walked out the door and stumbled onto a long line of patients all waiting to get in?"

"No," he shook his head with a smirk planted on his face.

"You heard a loud crash and ran outside to discover a wagon tipped over and saved the day rescuing all aboard?"

"No," again shaking his head.

"Ah, just tell me, please."

He let go of her and walked her to the table to take a seat.

"I just had a very nice chat with a Mrs. Geoffrey. She came just to invite us to dinner at their house this Friday."

Allie squealed. Frank covered his ears and let out a hearty laugh.

"Oh, I'm so excited! This will be fun!" Allie's mind was spinning in circles. "Will it just be us or is it a get together of some sort?"

"I'm pretty sure it's just us. She didn't make it sound like it was something other than dinner to meet the new folks."

Allie smiled and exhaled.

"Oh, what should I bring?"

"As she was leaving, she said just to bring ourselves. She made a comment about seeing us a few times. I'm thinking she might be feeling a little guilty about not inviting us sooner."

"Oh, well she shouldn't. People are busy, and I've only

been here just a handful of weeks. We are just finally getting settled in. The timing is perfect."

Allie stood and took up where she left off with the potatoes.

Frank went and stood next to her. "You know, I love you."

"I love you, too."

"How are you doing with all of this: the move to a new place, not knowing anyone but me?" He grabbed a potato and another knife and began helping her.

Allie stopped mid peel.

"I'm doing all right. I've been through serious situations in the past. This seems like a breeze. Of course, having a friend close by to talk to will be wonderful. There are just some secrets to a woman's heart that can only be known to another woman. I could tell you, of course, and have most of it, but only a woman can really understand it."

Frank was hurt a little, but didn't let it show. He wasn't sure what she meant by that. Of course, he knew that she went through a horrible experience with the abuse and then the lost baby because of it. He hurt for her. He desperately wanted to make this new future as bright as possible for her but was at a loss how to do that. All he could do was just keep loving her and loving her he would. He placed a kiss on her temple and washed up his hands.

"I'll be headed back to the office now. I've had a few people stop by and I don't want to miss anyone else just in case."

Allie was lost in thought about the upcoming dinner. She was already daydreaming about Friday's dinner plans. This was just the thing she had been needing.

"Oh, I'm sorry Frank, what did you say? I was in my own world for a moment."

He gave a little smile wishing he could be in that world with her. He wanted to understand her better. "Just that I was headed back to work."

"Oh, ok. I'll be here," she gave a soft chuckle and sigh.

Frank headed back to the office and picked back up where he left off with his letter to Doc Leman. He couldn't figure out Allie right now, but maybe he could at least get some answers about someone else Allie cared deeply for.

CHAPTER 8

Allie was so excited awaiting the day that she was having trouble sleeping. Friday was here, and she was dressing in her nicest dress while, Frank was downstairs waiting for her. She needed this night to go well.

A friend, someone to talk to, would bring so much comfort to her. Even in her darkest months, over a year ago now, she had her neighbor to talk with. Out of fear, she waited until Eddie had left for work. Those few hours they spent together chatting over a coffee helped her get through the worst days of her life.

She, of course, didn't have to deal with those issues now. Frank was a dream come true. Talking about the past and what her heart still struggled with would help her grow. She wasn't ready to talk with Frank about all of that. She needed someone who could understand her, like only another woman could.

Allie walked downstairs and into the front room where

Frank was sitting writing in a journal. He had several and they all were to be used for different patient cases. One was on skeletal issues, another pregnancy, there was one for general illness and gout. He had one for each type of issue he had treated in the past. He said they were to help him with future cases. When someone came in he could grab the journal that best fit the current situation and use what he'd learned from the past to help with the current issue.

He closed his book and stood when he noticed her.

"You look stunning"

"Oh, stop. I look the same as always, only the clothes are different."

"Well, that purple really sets off the green in your eyes. I love it," he said as he walked to her, took her blushing cheeks in his hands, and kissed her soundly.

Allie melted for a moment, then she pulled away.

"We should go so we aren't late."

She walked passed him and headed to the door. Frank followed behind. Once out, he helped her into the wagon and arranged the blanket over her lap. He then took his place on her left and sent the wagon into motion.

The Geoffrey house was just outside of town. It didn't take but a few minutes to get there. The home was made from logs. It was a small one story with a chimney that rose from the center made from rock. The Geoffrey's were an old pioneer family and this home was the homestead. Frank helped Allie down and together they walked to the wooden door.

Isabelle opened the door and welcomed them in. The home was small with a kitchen table in the center of the main room, a couple of rocking chairs along the outside wall, a stove in the back corner, and two doors on either side of the fireplace that led presumably to bedrooms.

"Welcome Mr. and Mrs. Hubbard! I'm Mrs. Geoffrey and this is my husband Mr. Geoffrey, but people just call us William and Isabelle, or Bill and Belle for short."

Allie thought Bill and Belle was cute.

"It's very lovely to meet you. I'm Alice, or Allie, and this is Frank."

The men shook hands.

"Dinner is almost ready. Please, make yourselves comfortable. I'll have it on the table shortly," Isabelle stated and walked back to the stove.

"Is there something I can do to help?" Allie asked.

"Oh, no dear. I'm treating you tonight. Go have a seat, please," she coaxed, pulling heavenly smelling biscuits out of the stove.

Allie sat down at the table and waited. The men took the seats along the wall and were hitting it off already. Bill was talking about the history of the area and Frank was hanging on every word, hungry for the information.

The Geoffrey's were older than she and Frank. They looked to be somewhere around their later forty's. Bill was a tall man, but was at ease in this small home. Belle was shorter than

Allie, but not extremely short. She held her silvery hair in a tight bun close to the nape of her neck. She was plump, but not overly so. Her eyes were kind.

Belle placed a pot of stew and the biscuits on the table. The whole home smelled of rosemary and garlic. Allie's mouth was watering. It was a humble meal, but judging by the smell it was bound to be delicious.

"Dinner is served. It's nothing fancy. We are not fancy folks. But it fills you up and warms your belly here in the coldest of days. Thank goodness those are behind us for yet another year. Yakima can get bitter cold in the deep winter and sweltering hot in the mid-summer. Right now, is the happy medium time when you can enjoy the sunshine on your face during the day, but still scoot up to the bone warming coals in the evening."

Belle took her seat closest to the stove. Bill made his way to the other end of the table and Frank sat opposite Allie.

"So, Frank, Allie, what brings you to Wiley City?" Bill spoke as Belle started serving the stew.

Allie looked to Frank. "Allie and I come from Deer Lodge, Montana. We went to school together. Shortly after finishing, I moved to the Portland area and earned my doctorate. Worked a bit in the area before making my way back home and reconnecting with Allie. Not quite a year later we were married and looking for a place to start my own practice. Many areas out this way are growing quickly, but this area stuck out at me as the perfect place for us. So, we came."

"That's a wonderful story. Bill and I were born in this

area. Our families were original settlers. This very cabin belonged to Bill's parents and where he grew up. We have now raised our own children here. One has stayed close by, Martha, but our two boys headed to Seattle. They wanted an adventure, I guess."

"Martha married a great guy and lives in Prosser, east of here," Bill talked through a bite of biscuit. "How is the practice coming, Frank?"

Frank put his spoon down and finished his bite.

"Dinner is delicious, Belle." He gave her a smile before turning his attention to Bill's question. "It started off pretty slow. I moved out here first and once I had a home for us, I wrote for Allie to join me. After she arrived, we quickly worked to do a little remodeling to make a private area to run the practice and picked up my orders for some essentials. I just opened a handful of weeks ago. With business starting really slow, we took a drive over to Ahtanum and passed out some cards Allie made to help spread the word. The following week traffic picked up a bit and seems to continue to grow."

"That's great news. There are some doctors in these parts, but having you close by is a blessing. Sometimes you are just too sick or things are too urgent to have to head to North Yakima." Bill stated, scooping a second helping into his dish.

Allie was enjoying her meal and watching the interactions between the other three. She was thankful that Frank didn't give away anything of her past. She would share that information when she was good and ready to those whom she chose to share it.

"Allie, dear, tell me a bit about you," Belle urged, playing hostess and including all her guests to join the conversation.

Allie set her spoon down and folded her hands in her lap finishing her last bite.

"Right now, I'm enjoying being a doctor's wife, but I will back up a bit. Around the same time Frank left for his schooling I started working at a restaurant in town. I waited tables for a while to help my folks out financially. My parents are farmers. I have a brother, Andrew. He suffered an injury several years ago and now will always be a child in his mind." Allie stopped afraid she perhaps should have kept that back.

"Oh, dear, I'm so sorry to hear that. Your parents must have been devastated." Belle placed her hand on the table close to Allie.

"They were originally. Pa had great dreams for his son someday taking over the farm. They have settled to the new path that is before them, though, and are very thankful he is still with them. He is a sweet boy. I miss him dearly."

"Your parents sound like good folks," Bill commented.

Allie never saw a man eat so fast. She continued eating, feeling a bit rushed by it. Belle was still enjoying her food at a leisurely pace and that helped to calm Allie. The rest of the meal finished with little more of Allie's past and mostly with small talk.

The Geoffrey's wanted to make sure the Hubbard's knew as much as possible of this area, its history and people. Dinner was pleasant and, when finished, Allie helped Belle clear the table. She had tea ready for the four of them to enjoy after dinner.

"It was a wonderful meal and I'm so happy to have met you both," Allie said as she and Frank stood to leave.

"Oh, heavens, I'm just sorry I didn't invite you earlier. Shame on me for not being neighborly," Belle chided herself as she walked them to the door.

Bill shook Frank's hand again. He seemed to be as genuine as Belle.

"Good to meet you. I'll come straight away should I need any doctoring. I'll make sure to help spread that word, too."

Allie and Frank left elated. They had made new friends in their new town.

CHAPTER 9

Flowers had been blooming for a couple of months. The fields were alive with yellow daffodils, blue and purple irises, dogwoods in shades from white to pink, and the fields of apple trees also joined the mix with branches covered in flowers. Baby bunnies, fawns, and other furry creatures could be seen playing here and there. The land was alive and thriving.

Allie loved every minute she could spend outside. Inside work was monotonous. She swept, dusted, washed the windows, kept up on the laundry, boiled the water and prepared the food. Without little hands causing dirt, though, she was basically just cleaning things that were already clean, aside from the laundry and cooking of course.

Frank had turned a small patch of land with a shovel and hoe he'd borrowed from the Wiley's. It wasn't a very big space, but it would do the job. After the garden was in, her front picket fence was next on the list. Frank would build it and she would paint it. That is, if he was able to find the time.

His patient numbers continued to grow. The practice

was off to a great start. Some people were able to pay and those who couldn't, traded. They were mostly given food items, which Allie appreciated. The more they received, the longer she could stay outdoors instead of in the kitchen.

Frank was concerned, knowing that not everyone was boiling their water like he preferred. He advised all his patients to do so. Some took his word seriously, others thought the way they had done things had been fine, and a change wasn't needed. Frank hoped they were right, but all signs pointed toward water being the culprit for the growing typhoid issue.

Frank and Allie were feeling more at home. There had been a handful more invites in the last weeks. Frank and Allie stayed busy many weekend nights, enjoying the company and hospitality of their neighbors. The people were good, hard-working folks, mostly.

The church ladies asked her to join the quilting group. Allie wasn't a skilled quilter, but she could do a decent basic job. She was excited to have something regular to look forward to and knew that her quilting skills would greatly improve with all the practice.

With the beauty of nature and the warm welcoming people around her, Allie still felt as though she was missing something. She knew just what that something was, but saying it out loud was still difficult.

She and Frank had climbed into bed for the night when she tried talking about it.

"Hon?"

"Hmmm yes." Frank replied, rolling over to face her.

"Uh, are you happy?" That wasn't exactly what she wanted to ask him, but maybe they could work up to it in this conversation.

"I'm very happy. Are you?" He propped his head up on his elbow.

"Yes, of course. Everything is nice here, but are you complete?" She sat up, really not sure how to say what she was thinking.

Frank sat up and scooted next to her. "I have you and that's all I need."

"Really? You don't want anything more?" She looked up at him.

"Of course, I would love to have a family, but if that doesn't happen, I'm great with just us." He put his arm around her.

"Frank it's been a while. We've been married for six months. Of course a little over a month we were apart, but... well, I never did talk to you about what Doc Leman said." She didn't want to because saying it out loud would mean it was real. She didn't want it to be real.

"Allie, I'm a doctor. And you know I found your file by accident when I was working for Doc."

"I know, but I don't know what you know." She shifted to face him.

"Ok, why don't you tell me in your words then, so I know what you need me to know."

Allie crawled out of bed and started pacing, her bare feet shuffling on the cold floor. She didn't want to talk about it, but knew it was time.

"So, Eddie thought I was doing something to prevent getting pregnant. He became angry. You know what happened when he was upset. What both of us didn't know, however, was that I was at that moment with child."

Frank stood, walked to her and embraced her softly stopping her from pacing.

"I know you know this, but I need to tell it straight through," Allie shrugged from his arms.

He looked in her eyes and gave her a gentle kiss on the lips.

"Ok, but you don't have to if you don't want to."

Allie closed her eyes and turned away, wiping tears as she talked.

"He killed our child. My body rejected it, but couldn't complete that. Doc Leman put me to sleep and did something, I don't even know what, you would probably know more than me where that's concerned. He said my body failed to remove everything and he had to help it. When I woke he told me that..." She caught a sob in her throat and cleared it to continue. "That I might not be able to carry any other children." She sat at the foot of the bed and wept into her hands.

Frank sat behind her and wrapped her up gently rocking her side to side.

"It's ok. I know, sweetheart. If we are supposed to have a family, God will provide. I know He will."

"How can you be so sure?" She questioned through sobs.

"He found a way to bring us together, right?" Allie nodded. "He never left your side through all of last year. So why would He leave you now?"

"I don't know. I just feel so broken," she confessed, working to regulate her breathing again. "I'm sorry. If I can't give you any children, I want you to know I'm sorry."

Frank stood up and picked her up. He carried her to the bed and laid her down. Then he crawled in and laid next to her.

"Don't be sorry. I know we will have a family, if it's in His plan. Things will work out. Just you wait and see."

They laid like that until she fell asleep. Allie wanted to believe him but wanting and doing were separate matters all together.

Frank had been wanting to know what had been on her mind. He knew she wasn't quite herself, but until she spoke, he couldn't have guessed what it was about. Of course he wanted children. He loved kids. She needed him to be strong. He would be happy with whatever future lay ahead. Or at least he would never let on otherwise. In truth he, too, would have to work on being content with the possibility of not having children. He would not let her see any struggles. She needed a rock and a rock he would be.

CHAPTER 10

Allie found herself sitting in a giant circle with women of all ages working on a large block quilt. The center block was larger than the rest and it had fancy flower designs in it. The flowers were in shades of pink and yellows. The rest of the blocks were green. Some had little leaves embroidered on them and others were plain. The blocks were first attached making long strips. The strips then were stitched together, making the full quilt. Once this portion was finished they would start on the backing. This would be a square block tied quilt when finished. They were working hard to finish it in time as a gift for an upcoming church wedding.

To Allie's right was Belle. She had spent a little more time with her over the last couple of weeks and they were becoming good friends. Belle was as old as her ma. She was a sweet soul with grit. Both she and Bill came from good people. Allie was glad to have found someone she could open up to, eventually.

On her left was Mrs. Wiley, the matriarchal head of the

group. The Wiley family ran the town as they were the original settlers to the area. It was a blessing to all that they were a good, honest, hard-working family.

The other women were various members of church. Emma sat on the other side of the table. She was closer to Allie's age and she hoped that she and Emma could become close friends soon. She and Frank hosted Emma and her husband, Roger, and children, Alex and Katie, a little over a week ago. Alex was not quite two, but already proving to be everything a two-year-old was known for. Katie was a big four-year-old young lady.

They had decided on a picnic lunch for the next outing. The children could run around and be kids while the adults supervised yet could still visit.

As Allie sat with the women, her thoughts turned to many subjects. The weather was growing warmer by the day and the sunshine on Allie's face was a welcome relief. It was a new year. A fresh start and Allie thought that God really wouldn't make two bad years in a row, *would He*? She hoped not. Her poor heart couldn't handle another one if it came anytime soon.

Conversation stayed light. The ladies talked about the weather and who had their crops seeded. Some excitement was had during talks of the tiny apples beginning to form as the blossoms were dropping. Allie didn't know much about apple farming, but knew it was a big deal in this area.

Orchards were everywhere irrigation was, and more trees were being planted over the winter. From the talk of the town regarding their apples, she was anxiously waiting to try one fresh off the tree. She'd had apples before, of course, but these farmers made their apples sound heavenly. Unfortunately, apple harvesting was in the fall, so Allie would have to wait much longer than her taste buds wanted.

"You haven't eaten an apple until you've eaten a Yakima apple," Belle had told her a while back.

Before she knew it, their hour of quilting was over, and it was time to pack up and head for home. The quilt wouldn't take too much longer to finish and then they would move onto the next.

Allie found Frank in his office between patients.

"Hi Allie," he gave her a quick peck and sat back down over his notes. "How was the quilting group?"

"It was more fun than I thought it would be. The ladies here are sweet and kind."

"Did you get a chance to mention about boiling water? I've been telling all my patients, but if you were spreading the word that would be helpful."

Allie didn't realize she should.

"Oh, I'm sorry. No, I didn't say a word. I guess public health would be part of my role as the doctor's wife, though. I'll bring it up next week."

"Thanks so much. More cases have cropped up and even though work is being done to try to clean up the city, it isn't slowing the disease down. I don't think it is the city's fault, though. Those who are getting sick aren't just from the city. It seems to hit at random all over here. There has to be a connection, but no one has been able to find it yet."

"Should I be doing more than just boiling water? I'm not sure what, but maybe there is something more for all of us to do?" Her brows were worried and Frank realized when he looked at her that he frightened her.

"No, no. I think that's all for now." Changing the subject on purpose, he reached for an envelope on his desk. "You got a letter today."

Allie took the letter and read that it was from her Ma.

"How exciting! I'll let you get back to work and take this into the kitchen to read."

Frank was curious what was in it. He hoped it would either say she was much improved or go into more detail about her illness. He refrained from reading it though. Hopefully Allie would fill him in completely.

Allie quickly left Frank and headed straight for the kitchen table. She took her gloves off and opened the envelope taking the folded paper out, unfolding it and laying it in front of her.

My Dearest Allie,

I hope this letter finds you happy and enjoying your life with Frank. Our spring weather seems to be fairly normal for this time of year, unlike last year. I continue to pray we never have a year like we did last.

The scorching sun, tinder dry land, and massive fire that destroyed so much is more than anyone can deal with more than once.

Drew misses you, but is falling into a new routine since you left. Adjusting takes a while for him, but he eventually figures it out. He is a great help around here.

Your Pa is just as stubborn as ever. His knee has been bothering him lately and I keep trying to get him to relax a bit and rest it, but you know him. He will keep going until he can go no more.

As for me, my dear, I'm still working towards getting better. Doc has been here several times and tells me to keep doing what I'm doing, which is rest, plenty of fluids, and your grandmam's bone broth. Blinne has been here a few times to help out, too. Did you put her up to that?

I should have known if I told you about this you'd find a way to help out. That is in your nature. She has been a blessing, catching us up on laundry and helping with cooking. Thank you for that. Hopefully, the next letter I send will be able to tell you that I'm fully recovered. I wish doc could tell me *what is going on. He still thinks it's just a virus, though, and we have to believe that and keep treating it like that. I love you, my sweet girl, and look forward to when either you two come to visit or your pa and I can come see you.*

Love Always,

Ma

Allie folded the paper and stuffed it back into the envelope. She needed to tell Frank. Something wasn't right and she was getting scared. She knocked on the door to his office. He opened the door a crack.

"Allie, is everything all right?"

"You should probably read it," she stated handing him the letter.

"I will. I have a patient here, so I'll come find you in a bit, okay?"

Allie nodded her head and ran to their room to write another letter.

Frank found her sitting at the little desk along their bedroom wall.

"I read the letter."

Allie turned at the sound of his voice.

"What do you think Frank?"

He walked to the bed and sat down on the edge.

"Well, it's difficult to decide. It could be any number of things from an illness that has to run its course, anemia maybe, but that doesn't completely fit... I don't know. Without being there and seeing for myself, it's too hard to tell."

"Do you think I should go? I have Blinne helping out, but I think she might need me. Blinne can't do it all. She has her own family that needs her."

"I really just don't know yet. I should have told you, I sent a letter to Doc a while ago. I'm not sure why I haven't heard from him yet. If you want to go, I understand. I think waiting a bit to hear from Doc, or maybe more information from your mom, would be a good idea too. It's really up to you."

Allie thought about it. She was needed in both houses. Frank could do everything on his own, but she was his wife and she didn't want him to have to do her duties. Both her parents could use help, too. She felt like she had to make an impossible decision.

"Waiting, I guess, wouldn't hurt... if it's not too long," she stated and stood in front of him, tipping her head down on his shoulder.

"Oh, Allie, come here," Frank urged then wrapped her up in his arms once she sat on his lap. "Your Ma is a strong woman. We will just pray that whatever this is isn't stronger than she is. Keep the faith, sweetheart. God's will be done."

That was easier said than done for Allie, but she would try.

CHAPTER 11

Allie woke the next morning needing fresh air. She dressed and made breakfast for Frank so he could start his day. Then she found herself aimlessly wandering around Wiley. There really wasn't much traffic, either. It was a sleepy town, and Allie loved the peace that it brought her. It meant she could think without being interrupted.

The town wasn't very big, and one could only wander so far before they came to the end. So, she turned and headed the other direction. She passed by the livery and stopped in to say a quick hi to their horse Penny. She didn't have anything to offer her and felt sad she didn't bring a treat. She borrowed the brush and brushed her down instead. Then she gave her a kiss on the nose and continued on her walk.

Just out of town there was a small creek. Back home she had a creek out the back of her house. Anytime she needed to think, recover from a broken heart, or just relax, she would go wade or just sit by the creek. She knew this one was on private property, but didn't think the Wiley family would mind if she plunked her feet in just by the road. She wouldn't make a habit of this until she asked permission first though. She needed to remember that the next time she saw Mr. Wiley.

Making her way down the slight hill she sat at the water's edge. After scanning the area to make sure she was alone and wouldn't be seen she unlaced her boots, removed her stockings and dipped her toes in. The days were warm, but the water was still very cold. Her feet felt like they were burning at first, but soon acclimated to the icy temperature. The water flowing over her taking her pain or worries with it was always soothing. She closed her eyes and just felt the water until her feet went numb and she realized she should probably pull them out of the water. She tucked her feet under her and let her body warm them back up. The tingling was a bit irritating and she wiggled her toes to hurry it along.

"Allie is that you?"

Allie startled and lifted her head off her knees. Standing in the road above her was Belle.

"Oh, hello, Belle. How are you?"

Belle walked down to Allie and decided to sit a spell next to her.

"I'm doing well, dear. How are you?'

"I'm all right. Just thinking." She looked out over the water and Belle followed her gaze.

"The water is a bit cold yet, isn't it dear?" Belle noticed Allie's boots and stockings placed next to her.

"It does have a bite, yes ma'am."

Allie knew it wasn't proper to be in any state of undress in public, but Belle wouldn't mind seeing her legs as she replaced her stockings and laced up her boots.

Allie was working to put herself back to rights, but Belle could see that she was still mentally somewhere else.

"Is there anything you'd like to talk about?" Belle asked, offering to listen.

Allie hesitated. She really didn't know Belle all that well, but out of those she knew here Belle was the closest, aside from Frank, of course. If she would tell anyone it would be Belle.

"My Ma isn't doing so well."

Belle sat waiting for more that didn't come. She would need to push a little for it. "What do you mean by well, dear? Is she sick?"

Allie sighed. "It appears so, but no one really knows what is going on. Doc is treating it like a virus, but she's been sick for several weeks now. She should at least have improvement if not be fully healed by now, I would think."

Belle scooted closer to Allie.

"So, you are worried, maybe a bit frightened?"

"Yes. I don't know what to do," Allie picked up a pebble beside her and tossed it into the creek.

"Well has she asked you for help?"

Allie chuckled. "My Ma asking for help? Then I would know, wouldn't I. She is a strong woman who doesn't like to burden anyone else with her problems. Both my parents are that way."

"Well then, I think you have your answer, dear."

Allie looked confused.

"It isn't time yet for you to go. You will know when it is. When your Ma loses the parts that make her who she is, that's when you know. Hopefully, whatever this is, she will pull out of. But, if a day comes when her spark dims, her character changes... that will tell you. Let's hope and pray it doesn't come to that, shall we?"

They grabbed hands and rose Allie's worries to God.

"Now you just remember to include Him in your worries you hear?"

"Yes, ma'am. Learning to lean on God has been something I've been working on for a while now. I always just want to jump into action instead of waiting for him. That's got me in a pickle a time or two before." She stared back at the water.

"I know you have a story, dear, and I'm ready and waiting whenever you want to talk about it. I know you will open up in your time, when it feels right. I won't push you. I have a mother's heart and will share a bit with you, if you want it."

Allie's eyes teared up and a lump formed in her throat. She batted her eyes to clear them.

"Oh dear, come here."

Belle embraced Allie as all of those pent-up tears fell. Tears for her past, for her ma, for her angel, for children she hoped to have one day. All things she had already cried over countless times. She wondered if she would ever have a healed heart. She gave Belle everything without telling her anything. One day maybe she would be strong enough to say the words. Today just having a shoulder to cry on was enough. Allie released first and worked at drying her eyes.

"Oh, look at me. I'm a mess."

Belle smoothed Allie's brown hair that had frizzed out a bit.

"You are beautiful, dear child. We all have hurts in our hearts. One can't go through this life without picking up a few. Life would be pretty boring otherwise." They both chuckled. "I'm here for you whenever you need me. Come on. Let's get you home."

They helped each other up and Belle walked Allie back to Frank and their home. Her heart was lighter. Sharing helped release a bit of her fears. Hopefully soon, she would be able to share more with Belle. She could use a day with Blinne, but Belle could become a good stand in. There was just something about talking out ones problems with another female. The hearts connected and they would understand more than was said. For now, she would take comfort in knowing she had gained a true friend here that she could lean on.

CHAPTER 12

Frank had a busy morning. He was thrilled that his practice was doing so well. Most patients came for little things: digestion issues, sprains, and the occasional sore tooth. His routine was settling in nicely. Spare time was becoming nonexistent and he loved that most days.

Each day he woke in the morning to his beautiful bride next to him. Together they rose and she prepared breakfast while he dressed and prepared for his day. They ate and then he was off, not seeing her again until lunch. Then he would go back to his office for a few more hours to finish out the day before joining her again for dinner. There were some empty times here and there that he could pop out and see her briefly. He loved those times when he could surprise her. Being busy was a blessing, as they needed a steady income, but he missed those first few weeks when he could spend the whole day with her.

Frank didn't know what she did all day to occupy her time. Obviously, she cooked. And she cooked well, based on his expanding stomach. He needed to cut back on the amount of food he ate. He also knew she was in the quilting club and was excited for her to have something to do that would get her out of the house and visiting with community members, even if it was just once a week. She did go visiting with a few new friends. He was aware there were probably many hours of nothing to do. He hoped that that would change soon. Allie was never one to sit around doing nothing. If she wasn't helping her parents, she was out looking for or working a job to help provide.

Today as he was driving out to a bed bound patient's home, he wondered just what Allie was up to. After the fact, he thought she might like to come with him. He would need to remember to ask her if she wanted to join him in the future.

This particular patient was an elderly man who broke some ribs and a hip from falling off his roof trying to repair it. Pneumonia had set in and it wasn't looking promising. This was the part of the job he hated. Losing patients regardless of age was hard. Even harder was telling the family it was time to say goodbye.

Some doctors were able to turn off their emotions and somehow not let it affect them. Frank was not one of those doctors. He loved, laughed, and cried right along with everyone he treated and their families. Having the title of doctor gave many people unrealistic ideas about your abilities. Every doctor was still human, still made mistakes, and had limitations on their knowledge and skills.

There would always be those patients who couldn't be treated. The medical field was exploding with new information all the time on how to treat various ailments. No matter how fast the medical community worked to learn more, the diseases always seemed to be one step ahead. Or in many cases, ten steps ahead.

Typhoid was one of those that grated him. Despite having many women's groups and other clubs begin working late last summer to start the cleanup of the city, which was obviously an ongoing project, and having a three-month field study done, nothing had changed. Then they placed a regional health officer in the area who continued the cleanup education and issued warnings to those who failed to comply.

Even with all of those things in place, cases were increasing. Frustration was putting Frank's feelings mildly. He felt as though they were racing an avalanche that would overtake them at any moment. Being overly dramatic was something he was not known for, but he hoped that was all it was.

He slowed his horse and hopped down from the wagon, taking his bag with him. Elizabeth Dodd was at the door waiting, a worried expression on her face.

"Good day ma'am. How is John doing?"

She stepped aside and let him enter.

"There hasn't been improvement."

Another patient told him about this elderly couple. Frank showed up on his own, deciding someone should help. He'd been there twice before and he wasn't charging anything for his time. Elizabeth would be put through enough fairly soon. She didn't need a bill from him hanging over her head also.

"I'll go take a look. I'll only be a minute."

Frank headed back to the same room he had visited both times before. John was laying propped in bed, asleep.

Frank started by checking his broken bones which had made no improvement. On a prior visit, he'd bound the man's chest, but with his advanced age, the bones just didn't like to heal.

Broken ribs were a perfect set up for pneumonia. Anything that would make an elderly person laid up in bed for a length of time could bring the disease on. Having bound ribs restricting the chest movement only increased the probability.

Frank took out his stethoscope and listened to John's lungs. He didn't like what he heard, but there was nothing to do to change it. John's left lung was completely full of fluid. His right partially. His breathing was labored and fever was high. It was only a matter of time. He had already told Elizabeth what to expect. She was aware that John would die. How long it would take was the question that remained.

Frank left the room and found Elizabeth sitting at the table. He sat down next to her and placed his hand on her back. She didn't need him to voice it as she already knew it was close. Frank closed his eyes and prayed out loud for God to show mercy and take John quickly so his suffering would be short.

"Keep giving him the medication I gave you, but let's double it." Frank wouldn't tell her that this would help him go quicker. "You send for me if you need anything?"

Elizabeth nodded through her tears and cleared her throat.

"Thank you, doctor."

"No thanks needed. I'm sorry. If there was anything I could do, I would."

She nodded as tears slipped down her face. Frank embraced her and held her tightly.

"Are your kids on their way?"

She let go and walked to the window. Her arms folded across her chest holding herself up. "Bobby is here. He ran an errand for me and will be back anytime." Bobby lived close and Frank was relieved to know she wasn't alone. "Melissa and Annie are on their way but Gloria, our baby, can't come out. She is ready to deliver any day with her third and didn't want that to happen on a train."

Frank stood next to her.

"It will be good to have family with you. Decisions will need to be made soon. Please let them help you. If you have any questions or need help, come find me. I'm not far. Allie and I will do what we can." Frank hated having to leave her, but he needed to get back to the office. "I'm so sorry, Elizabeth. I wish I could do more."

"No, you have done enough. I will be fine. We've always known something would eventually take us. Everyone has to pass. John has lived a long good life. We've had many years together. I will cherish every one of them until it is my turn to join him. This is difficult, but I will get through this as everyone else has had to do before me." Elizabeth affirmed, her voice faltering a bit.

Frank squeezed her one more time and walked back to his wagon. He hated leaving her. She was putting on a brave face, but her heart was shattered. Life had too many disappointments. The hope was that one could have just as many or more blessings to balance it out. Unfortunately, for many that wasn't the case. He hoped John and Elizabeth had balance.

Driving home, he decided to check the post. Maybe there would be good news from his parents or friends that could help cheer him up. The only letter at the post was from Doc which sent him racing for home to Allie.

Frank rushed through the door with a look on his face that stopped Allie in her tracks. She had been sitting with Emma enjoying a cup of tea. Allie looked at Emma and Emma rose thanking her for the tea and excused herself.

Allie knew something was wrong before he ever showed her the letter. Doc had answered Frank's questions. Allie's mother was dying. Cancer. Based on the lump that was thought to be a virus attacking her lymph nodes, the cancer had already spread.

Belle's words before about knowing when the time was right played back in her mind. It was time. She had to go now. She was just there a few short months ago. Everything seemed fine.

How could someone go from healthy and living life to dying in a matter of months?

Allie had no answers. She was riding the train home alone. Frank couldn't leave his practice so early in its start. He desperately wanted to go. Dealing with this was something Allie shouldn't have to do on her own, but given the circumstances, Frank felt his hands were tied.

So, Allie sat in a metal box, bumping and jostling

towards Montana so she could help her Ma finish with this world and her Pa pick up the pieces and somehow move on. She didn't know if she had the strength it would take, but she had no choice.

The ride was non-eventful. The view was close to the same as the trip out a few months ago. The only difference was the lush green of the countryside. Before, it was all white. Now life bloomed everywhere.

Ironic that her Ma's life was dimming, shriveling, as so much new was forming. The timing was odd. It felt off. She felt as though she had walked into a parallel world. Everything around her was the same, behaving as it should, but nothing was the same. The spring green seemed darker to her. The sounds were muffled. People were moving faster and slower at the same time all around her. Her life had turned upside down and inside out and she didn't know how to move forward from here.

Allie was trying to mentally prepare herself. Thoughts were circling in her head.

Would Ma look different? Would she want her there? Was there anything she could do for her? Would Pa want her there? Was Pa dealing with it or avoiding the inevitable? And Drew, what did he know? Was he ok? What would happen after for him?

So many questions with no answers. Allie couldn't do anything. She wasn't eating or sleeping. She just stared out the window as the thoughts and questions circled in her mind.

The train arrived in Deer Lodge on time, although Allie

wouldn't have known if it was early or late. She wasn't even clear on the day. The train was emptying and the sidewalk was filling up. Looking out the window she could see the only familiar face she wanted to at the moment. The rest of the crowd was faceless bodies moving in all directions.

Her Pa was waiting for her this time. Frank sent a telegram ahead of her arrival. Allie rushed to Pa and he held her up as she lost control. Standing at the station in front of everyone, she felt as if it was just the two of them together. People were walking past, staring, curious, but she had no knowledge of them.

Pa had moved her to the wagon and lifted her up. He left her briefly so he could get her things. Then they were off silently heading towards the future Allie didn't want to see, but had no choice. Life was dishing this out whether she liked it or not. Now was the time to face this head on and find the strength within her that her ma possessed and passed on to her. It was time to be the rock for her Ma as her Ma had always been for her. The hat was being passed whether she was ready or not. She just hoped she could make her ma proud for the last time.

CHAPTER 13

Frank moved through his days in a haze. Allie was two states away dealing with things she shouldn't have to without him. He should be there. He kept telling himself that, yet he couldn't figure out how to make that work. He had patients he couldn't just up and leave. Life couldn't be simple. He knew she had support of friends and family all around her. They all would be in a cocoon, in a way. His parents were there as well. She could lean on them, but it wouldn't be the same.

Life was forever changing for Allie, and he was supposed to be the one she leaned on in times like this. He could take a vacation without repercussions had his practice not been so young. Word was still spreading, and patient traffic was steadily picking up. He didn't want to up and leave for those needing him to find an empty office. Their future demanded that he stay here and strengthen his practice. Otherwise, all he and Allie had done so far might be for naught.

Frank's morning continued with a handful of patients coming by. A few were repeat for continuing problems and a couple were new, continuing to secure the thought of him needing to stay here instead of heading to Allie.

A pregnancy he was following was progressing how it should, a sore tooth he was thinking would need pulled, but the patient was refusing at this point, and a sprain that kept a farmer off his foot and upset with Frank for not being able to do his work.

Many people chose to direct their frustrations at the doctor. Frank was used to that and didn't take any of it to heart. He knew when the foot had healed the relationship would improve.

He skipped lunch forgetting to eat. Without Allie cooking at defined points in the day he lost track of the time. His stomach told him he needed to eat something, though, so he took some time and prepared a meal that he could eat later for dinner as well. While he was eating someone knocked on his door.

"Hi Doc. My Ma sent me to let you know it happened," Bobby said, his hat spinning in his hands.

Frank had seen it many times, saying the word died was hard for most. It was more final to speak it.

"Hi Bobby, why don't you come in a minute. Have a seat."

They both took seats. Bobby was a decent sized man, but today, he was a smaller version of himself.

"I know it hurts, but he isn't in any pain anymore. There is some comfort in that, even if it's small," Frank spoke practiced words, staring at the wall and forcing himself back into this moment. "Does Elizabeth have a plan for now? She can't run that orchard on her own."

Bobby coughed to clear his throat and shook his head slightly.

"We are still working on the details. All us kids have our own lives and moved on from here. I think she will have to sell and move in with one of us. She can decide which one though. We all have different lives. Some of us have kids just about grown and then there is Gloria who is still welcoming new in. I don't know if she will want to go to a quieter home or one still very active and busy. Maybe she will spend a little time with all of us until she decides."

Frank took a deep breath.

"That might be the best option. I know things probably need to move fairly quickly now, but please try to take as much time as you can. She will need time to process all of this."

Bobby stood and put on his hat.

"We will. Thanks again, Doc. I better get back out there. We are taking turns making sure she isn't ever alone."

"That's probably best for now. Take care and don't hesitate if you need anything."

Frank watched Bobby walk away. He knew this would happen. He actually hoped it would come sooner than it did. John held out a while longer than most. He thought he would feel more than he did. He was numb. At least John wasn't in pain. Frank saw to that. He hoped that Allie's ma was also not suffering, but again he had no way of truly knowing since he wasn't there.

He went through the rest of the routine by memory. Somehow he managed to treat all his patients, eat dinner, and make it to bed without realizing he even did it. Yet, there he was, laying on his side of the bed with a cold empty place next to him. He wanted to go, he just didn't know how to make that work without causing problems for his practice.

Frank was more torn than he had ever been before. His body was here in Wiley City going through the motions, but his mind traveled with Allie to Deer Lodge. He wished he could know everything that was going on over there. After several hours of tossing and turning he finally fell asleep without resolving that problem.

CHAPTER 14

Ma was propped up in bed with a closed book in her lap. She had a weak smile on her face. Allie walked to the bed and knelt beside it, holding Ma's hands in her own. They stared at each other for a minute or two before Ma took one hand and cupped Allie's face.

"Hello, my sweet girl."

"Hi, Momma."

The house was quiet. Pa was outside and had Drew with him. Allie saw Drew when she first arrived. He was withdrawn. He had gone inside himself and chose to hide there. His whole world was turning on end and no one knew how to help him.

"So, you couldn't deal without me here, huh?"

Allie was trying to make a very difficult meeting as light as possible. Instead of chuckling they both just sighed and stared at each other.

They stayed in silence for a long time. Each holding the other. No one wanted to speak of the truth that permeated the air. Work had gone undone all around them. Ma's bright cheery yellow curtains had a layer of dust dulling their color. Her sheets smelled of undeniable sickness. Washing those would be first on her to do list. Now was not the time to weep. Work needed doing and she came to help. Using her hands to do things would help get her through this.

She started in the bedroom, making it fit once again for her Ma. Just because she was dying didn't mean she needed to lay in it Allie thought. Her next stop was the kitchen. Her pa had certainly been trying. He was just one person, though, and he couldn't stay on top of his chores and Ma's.

Allie cleaned up the dishes, wiped down the table, and set to work making something for supper. Once that was simmering, she moved to the front room and tidied that up as well. Tomorrow she would tackle the laundry and make some bread. She felt as though she was doing something useful, something that helped everyone.

Drew walked in and went straight for his room. She had helped everyone but Drew. He was always an emotional person, but since the accident it was hard to decipher those emotions. Allie thought about following him, but decided giving him some time to come to her might be better. She chose to go sit with her Ma instead.

Ma had slept most of the day away. She assumed that would be the case. Frank filled her in on what to expect as much as he could. She caught a few things he said, but most of it was just noise that her brain refused to comprehend.

"How was your day, dear?"

Ma's voice shook her out of her thoughts.

"Oh, busy. I got this place back into shape and have soup simmering if you're hungry."

"Not right now. I'm not very hungry yet. Thank you for the work today. I can't seem to stay up on all of it anymore."

"Of course not. And no one expects you to."

"I sleep most of the time now."

"Are you in any pain?" Allie wished she was a doctor. Then maybe she could do something more to help her.

Ma smiled sadly.

"Some yes. Doc is doing what he can and Pa makes sure I take my medications."

"That's good. And you should get your rest. It'll keep your strength up."

Ma laughed.

"What good is strength, dear? I can't do anything. I'm just lying here waiting for God to take me home."

Allie put her hand on her mouth and fought back tears.

"Oh, come here. I shouldn't talk like that to you."

Allie laid on the bed with her Ma.

"It's true, though. I was so hopeful this was just a virus,

but I think I knew from the beginning. Something was just off. It didn't feel the same. I had a gut feeling, but I desperately wanted to be wrong. Then doc voiced his suspicions. At first I didn't believe him. He could be wrong, but I keep getting worse. I could go to the city and have some tests run, but I know they will just say the same thing Doc is saying. I have come to terms with it for myself. I have Drew to take care of, though. What am I to do about that? Everyone must someday face it. I just hope those that I leave behind don't suffer too much over me. I've had my ups and downs through the years, but it was a good life. You and Drew are my everything. I'm so proud of what you've become."

Allie laid there listening to her. She wanted to be quiet and just hear everything her Ma had to say. She would hold all of the words in her heart for after. They laid like that until Pa came in with a bottle and glass of water.

"Time for some medicine."

Allie stood and left the room so they could have some alone time. She decided it was time to find Drew. He was still up in his room. She walked in and he ignored her. Maybe he didn't really even see her. She put her hand on his shoulder and he shrugged it.

"Drew, I miss you. It's me, Allie."

"I know who you are."

She smiled. He spoke. That was something.

"Can I get a hello hug?" she held her arms out waiting.

"No."

She folded her hands around her stomach. She knew he didn't mean to, but that still hurt her. "Why?"

He stood and faced her raising his voice, "Because you're here. You came, that means Ma is dying. If you stayed home Ma wouldn't die. She would have to stay alive and do her work, but now you're doing it for her."

"Oh Drew. Is that what you think?" Allie sat at the foot of his bed.

"Yes, you need to go home so Ma can get better."

"Drew, please come sit down. Please?" He obliged her, but he didn't want to.

"Drew, it is true that Ma is dying, but she would die with or without me. My coming here hasn't changed anything"

"He started crying and stood, his face turning red.

"Yes, it did. If she has work to do, she has to get better. No one else can do it. You need to go home." He pointed towards his door and stomped his foot.

Allie stood.

"I will leave your room, but I'm not going home. Both Ma and Pa need me here. Neither one of them can keep up with this place and take care of Ma, too."

Allie closed the door behind her and heard her brother crying. She knew he was angry. It made no sense talking to him now with him being in this state. She knew he'd shut her out and it would be like talking to a wall.

Allie made her way down to sit by the fire. There was a pile of socks sitting in a basket and she realized they needed darning. She gathered the materials necessary and began tackling that task while letting the warmth of the fire warm her through to her bones.

Her mind wouldn't relax. She wasn't sleeping well with her mind racing. She worried Ma needed something at night and she wouldn't hear her. Pa was with her and she knew even though he was avoiding the subject during the day, he had to be helping her at night. She was thankful for that, at least.

All of this was temporary and once it was finished she knew she would miss everything. A bad day with Ma was still a day with her. She didn't think Ma was in pain, but realized if she was Ma might not have the same view as Allie did. She made a mental note to talk with Doc when he came next about pain management and made sure they were doing all they could in that area. Allie didn't want her Ma to hurt and if she did and there was nothing to be done about it she would, reluctantly, pray for a faster ending.

She finished the darning and grabbed the Bible on the table next to the chair randomly opening it to John chapter 16. She read through to verse 22 before stopping to ponder the text. God was telling her that even though she was experiencing great sadness that would only deepen in the next few weeks, she would one day find joy again.

Allie couldn't fathom when or how long that may take. She did take comfort in knowing one day it would. She knew everyone was destined to die, even if she felt she wasn't ready for her Ma to go. Those left behind had to deal with it and work their way back to living.

Allie would have to move past this and live again. The future joy would take work and she would take all the help God would provide, but knowing He wasn't asking anyone to do what He Himself didn't do helped somewhat. The pain of knowing what was to come and the great sadness she felt while watching her Ma grow closer to death everyday didn't abide, but she knew one day peace would come. It still hurt, but she had hope. Life did move on, somehow.

CHAPTER 15

The next several days were filled with people coming and going. Everyone wanted to bring food and see her mom. Allie was doing her duty accepting the guests and filtering those few in that Ma would want to visit with and sending others away, so they wouldn't disturb her sleep.

At some point Ma would probably want to see everyone, but she didn't have the energy for more than a few short visits a day. Doc had been here a couple of times and the news hadn't changed. She was dying and by the looks of it, not long from now. Part of Allie was happy knowing that she wouldn't suffer for very long, but the other selfish part wanted her Ma here as long as possible.

Allie was around the side of the house removing clothes from the line when she heard a knock at the door. She set Pa's shirt in the basket and walked around front to see who it was this time. When she saw the familiar red hair of her long childhood friend she started crying. Blinne walked to her and held her while the tears fell. They stood there a long time... holding each other, both crying, the laundry all but forgotten for the moment.

"Is there anything I can do to help? I feel so awful, Allie." Blinne broke the hug, but kept her hands on Allie's shoulders.

Allie used her apron to dry her tears.

"Nothing. There is nothing anyone can do, and it is such a helpless feeling. We are all just waiting. Pa doesn't really want to talk much about after right now. I guess we will deal with that when it happens. Ma seems sad but accepting of her own fate. She worries about all of us though. Drew thinks it's my fault. I tried to talk to him, but he isn't ready to listen. I don't know what to do."

"Grab your laundry and come on in, I'll make us some tea."

Blinne knew where everything was since much of her childhood was spent at Allie's house. The girls were closer to sisters than friends.

After Allie set the laundry down in the front room, she found Blinne in the kitchen. That's when she noticed her belly. Instead of being happy she felt jealous and angry and she hated herself for it.

"How are you feeling? You should sit and let me do that."

"Stop it, I'm fine. I'm at the good stage now. Sickness is gone, but I'm not so huge that I feel like an elephant," Blinne laughed at her own joke, but Allie just sighed sadly.

Allie sat down wondering how life could just go on. Her Ma was dying as her best friend was bringing in a new life. Allie was caught in the middle.

"How is Lena doing? Where is she?"

"I left her home with George. I wasn't sure a baby crawling around and making noise would be appropriate right now."

"I'm sure it would have been fine. I miss that chubby face. I'm sure she has changed so much in the few months I've been gone."

"You have no idea. They grow so fast," she handed a cup of tea to Allie and sat at the table with her.

"Tell me about Wiley City. And Frank," Blinne's eyes twinkled as she looked over the mug of tea.

Allie smiled and looked down into her cup.

"Wiley City is small. It's new, just getting started. Nothing like Deer Lodge. North Yakima is larger. It's not too far from us. The people so far are wonderful. I haven't met anyone I don't like, although I'm sure there will be some. With as many people that are there a few are bound to turn up. She paused to sip her tea. "Frank is doing well. His practice is really picking up and keeping him busy. I know he wanted to be here, but leaving so soon after opening is risky."

"That's awful that he couldn't come. I'm here for you. Anything you need."

Allie already knew she could count on Blinne. It was

nice to hear those words though.

"Blinne is that you?" Ma had somehow climbed out of bed and was standing at her door.

Allie rushed up and went to go help support her Ma. Blinne followed.

"I'm here."

"Allie, dear, will you make me a cup of tea too? Blinne, help me back to bed, please."

"Of course, Ma."

Allie headed back to the kitchen and Blinne wrapped Ma's arm around her shoulder. They walked to her bed and Blinne helped ease her down, adjusting her pillow just so.

"Thank you dear. Blinne, if you will, get into the bottom drawer in my dresser and find the journal. I would like you to take that home and hide it. After," Ma licked her lips and hesitated a moment before continuing. "Please give it to Allie. I don't want anyone else seeing it. Understand?"

"Yes, of course."

Blinne moved from the bed and quickly retrieved the journal. She was curious about what was in it, but would show respect and refrain from reading it herself. This was Allie's.

Allie made her way in and Blinne hid the book behind her back.

"I'm going to head for home, Allie. Your Ma is up. You should visit with her."

"Are you sure? I'm sure Ma wouldn't mind if you stayed with us." Allie set her cup of tea on the table beside the bed.

"I am."

Blinne walked to Allie, and with one arm hugged her. She kept the journal behind her back with the other. Then she turned and winked and smiled at Ma before she headed home.

CHAPTER 16

The days had grouped together to form a couple of weeks, and Frank was still just as lost. He put a note on the office door saying he would be back later in the day and decided to head to North Yakima to the Cascade Lumber Company to pick up some boards. He was going to work on the picket fence Allie wanted. Hopefully he would finish so when she came home she would have a little something good.

The mill sat northeast of the city. It was right next to the river and they used the water to float the logs. The weather decided to rain on him in his open wagon. It only amounted to a drizzle and didn't really concern him much. He did make a mental note that maybe he should rig something up to the wagon to protect Allie on days they had to go somewhere, and it was rainy.

The trip there and back was quick and easy. He parked in front of the house and dropped off the wood in the yard. Then he parked the wagon and brushed down his horse at the livery. On his way walking back home, someone he hadn't met before came running down the road. She turned and ran down his road. He picked up speed to see what that was all about, but first passed John Wiley, who stopped him to talk.

"Hey, Doc. How is the business going?"

"Hi, John. Things are going real good. It's getting pretty busy. I decided to take a half day or so off. Picked up some lumber. Allie really has her sights set on that picket fence we talked about before."

"How is Allie? I heard she had an emergency and had to head home."

"Yep, it's sad really. Her Ma has cancer and she needed to go help them out a bit. Hey, John will you walk with me. I just saw a woman running towards my place. Or at least that direction. I hope it's not for me, but I feel I should make my way back in case she needs some help."

"Sure thing. Hopefully it's nothing serious, but if it is maybe I can help, too."

They continued their conversation about Allie's Ma as they made their way back to the office. Sure enough, the girl was frantically pounding on both the office door and the front door.

"Ma'am can I help you?" Frank asked jogging up to her.

"Are you the doctor?"

"Yes, ma'am at your service."

"Oh, thank God! It's my mother. She isn't doing well."

"Annie is that you? My you've changed a bit," John

caught up to them.

"John, yep it's me. Please, we should hurry. Ma isn't good."

Frank couldn't remember an Annie. He knew he never met her before, but he was trying to figure out if he had heard the name. There was something there. He felt he should know it, but he just couldn't remember.

"My wagon is all hitched up around the corner. Let's all get in," John urged.

Annie started running in the direction the wagon would be and the guys followed. They weren't sure what this was about, but it seemed urgent. John drove and it was a good thing that he knew who Annie was and where they were headed since Frank was still at a loss. Then they pulled up at a familiar house, and it all fell into place. Elizabeth.

Frank took off running. He burst through the door and the rest of her kids directed him to the bedroom. Bobby explained she had collapsed and they got her into bed. She was unconscious. Frank quickly examined her, but realized he forgot his bag back at the office in the rush to leave, so was limited with what he could do.

Elizabeth was breathing, but barely. She was cold to the touch, but sweating profusely. Her lips were blue and Frank opened her eyelids to check dilation. That's when she retched on the floor. Frank quickly went through the symptoms and his heart sunk.

I took the meds back after John died right?

He was trying to remember back, but since Allie left everything blurred together. Mentally he was with her in Montana, but physically he was here. Treating people and apparently making big mistakes.

Frank was trying to decide what to do when she took that horrible sounding breath no doctor likes to hear from a patient he wants to survive. She was gone. He knew without even looking. Oh God, Oh God. What have I done? Frank's mind ran rampant.

John entered and closed the door behind him leaving the family out.

"John, I've made a huge mistake."

John's eyes were concerned. He looked at Elizabeth and could tell she was gone. She was turning more ashen by the second.

"What did you do?"

Frank was pacing.

"I was treating John before he died. I gave Elizabeth medicine to give him. Afterwards I forgot to collect the pills. She took them. She killed herself. Everything points to that. All of her symptoms match perfectly." Frank's legs gave out and he sat on the floor.

John processed what had just happened. He looked back and forth between Frank and Elizabeth.

"No, you did not kill her. Don't go thinking that way. She took those pills on her own. You've been mighty worried and your mind is elsewhere. It happens Frank. We are going to tell those kids she died of a broken heart. I've heard that before and it really isn't untrue. They don't need to be feeling any guilt from this."

Frank nodded but remained on the floor. "I'm a doctor. I'm supposed to know better."

"You are a doctor, and based on the talk spreading around here, you are a good doctor. Don't go letting one mistake change that. I think it's best for the time being, you take some time off. Go to Montana. Be with Allie. We need you focused and sharp when you come back and open back up."

"I'll lose business. People here need me now," Frank sighed and leaned his head against the wall.

"They need a doctor who can concentrate at the task at hand, and right now you can't do that. Don't worry about the people here. I'll pass the word around that a family emergency has come up and you will be back as soon as possible. Folks around here are good people, Frank. They'll understand. Give 'em some credit."

Frank sat motionless for minute thinking it all over and then he nodded and let John help him up.

"First we must find any medication left behind. Then you must go out there and tell them the truth. She had a broken heart. It just couldn't keep ticking any longer."

After a short search in the room they found the pill bottle. It was in her dresser and empty, as Frank suspected it would be. Frank's heart fell more.

Frank and John gathered the family and told them of Elizabeth's passing. The girls fell apart with the news. Bobby remained stoic.

Frank and John left them to their grief and good byes. John drove Frank home and the pile of wood in the front yard was all left and forgotten. Frank immediately packed, placed a note on the office door saying closed, but would re-open as soon as possible. He signed it apologetically. He couldn't think about what this might do for business. What would happen if word got out that his mistake killed a patient? He needed to leave. John drove him to the train station where he would stay as long as needed to catch the next train east out of town.

CHAPTER 17

As the days drew on, Ma weakened. Doc was coming daily now to check on her. He explained what they should expect over the next several days. No one knew for certain how long it would take. It all depended on how much of a fight she had left in her.

Allie absorbed the information and carried on as if losing a ma was a daily occurrence. Just another day: sweeping the floor, prepping the meals, changing soiled sheets, spoon feeding and holding a cup to Ma's mouth so she could drink because she was too weak to do it herself. All became normal everyday activities, but they weren't normal. Inside she was screaming, but outside she held herself together. She had no other choice.

Her Pa tuned out most everything. He refused to listen. He spent his days either laying with Ma talking about the past or outside doing anything and everything to not think about the inevitable.

Drew was still withdrawn, and Allie had no idea how to

bring him out of it. She worried more about what would happen with her brother afterwards. She wasn't certain if Pa wanted to stay here or if he could continue with Drew's care by himself. She hoped that Ma and Pa talked about that when he was with her.

Allie's mind kept wandering to the days ahead. Each time she would take a breath, shake her head, and bring herself back to the present. She needed to stay in this moment. The whole of the situation was too big to deal with at once. Taking each day as it came was the only way to stay focused and be able to handle everything as it came.

She longed to go to her spot, the creek, where she could wash her troubles away for a while. The creek was always there for her to do just that when she needed it. She knew this might just be too big for the creek to give her any rest. There was too much work to do for her to take any time out, so she just pushed on.

Blinne checked on Allie every day. She looked forward to her visit. For a brief moment, she could count on a change of subject. Ma was always present in their minds, but they could focus on something trivial for a few minutes.

Lena came some of the time. That little girl was a bright spot to everyone's day. Allie would set her next to Ma and Ma's eyes would sparkle, if only briefly, like a little bit of life would find its way back in them.

While Allie was happy to see those moments, it also brought sadness. Allie would never be able to see her ma interact with her child. Ma wouldn't know any potential future grandchildren. Then she would circle back to the possibility of never having children. She would never tell Blinne the battle of emotions that fought within her when Lena was around. That little girl was precious, and the pain it caused was Allie's cross to bear. She just hoped someday she could move past all of it and find happier times again.

The front door seemed to not stay closed for long. Someone was either entering or exiting. Allie let them all go in to see Ma now. Most of the time Ma was asleep and didn't know they were there. They all brought things, food mostly. Ma couldn't eat it and the rest of them usually were not hungry. The food sat and went to waste. People felt like they were being helpful, so she didn't say anything except thank you.

No one stayed long. Allie stayed out of the room when a visitor was there and wasn't sure if they spoke to her sleeping Ma or just stood there and stared at her. She assumed a little of both depending on the person. Crying was a constant for many who visited with Ma. Allie refused to allow herself to cry. She had to stay strong to keep the family going. If she broke down now she wasn't sure she could pull herself back up. That would have to wait until after.

This afternoon brought many visitors Allie had known her whole life, including Mrs. Wimble and her daughter Gladys, who was a school mate of Allie's. Gladys and her mother were noted for being the town gossips, but Gladys had seemed to have a change of heart and had turned her life around.

Mrs. Wimble desperately wanted Gladys and Frank to make a match, but after a strong pursuit in the end, it seemed that just wasn't what Gladys wanted all along. She was trying to please her mother and after a while decided to stop and do what she wanted to do. Mrs. Wimble went in to Ma's room and

Gladys sat at the table with Allie catching up.

"How are you holding up, Allie?" Gladys looked a bit nervous and was biting her lip.

Allie put on a sad, but reassuring smile.

"I'm all right. Ma is still fairly young, but Doc tells us that cancer knows no age. Everyone must die at some point, whether we are ready for it or not. It's sad. I'm going to miss her, but I don't want to see her hurting anymore."

"I completely understand that. Is there something I can do?" She was fidgeting with her hands.

Allie placed a hand on top of Gladys'.

"No, thank you. Your offer is very kind." Wanting to shift the conversation, Allie paused. "How are you? Any special someone?" Allie was sure when she gave up on Frank so fast last year someone else must have been in her sights.

"No, no one special," Gladys smiled. "I know my abrupt change last year left everyone to speculate what I was contemplating next, but I couldn't say anything until I knew for sure it would happen."

Allie was curious now. She was so sure there was someone else. If not someone then what? Allie stayed quiet and listened as Gladys continued.

"I'm going to become a teacher," she blurted with a wide smile on her face.

Allie put her hand on her chest.

"Oh, Gladys! I'm so happy for you. How exciting. Have you already started?"

"Not yet. I have exams to pass, which I am studying for. If I pass I will have a two year certificate for rural teaching. Papa is so happy for me. Mother thinks I'm losing my mind. She doesn't want her daughter working for a living. To her you are only successful if you have married a successful man," Gladys rolled her eyes.

Allie covered a chuckle.

"This is all so wonderful. I truly am happy for you. I wish you the best."

Mrs. Wimble stepped out of the room.

"Thank you, Allie, for allowing me to spend some time with her. Gladys are you ready?"

Gladys stood and rolled her eyes to Allie.

"Yes mother."

Allie stifled another chuckle.

"Thank you for stopping in. I understand Gladys is working towards becoming a teacher. That is exciting news."

Mrs. Wimble failed to hide the disgust in her voice.

"Yes, I suppose it is. Come along, dear. We must be on our way."

Gladys looked back and gave Allie a brilliant smile. Allie pushed in the chairs at the table and went about her day. Having friends stop in brightened her mood briefly. After they left it went straight back to a heavy gloom that hung like fog in every room.

Even though she knew why Frank needed to stay in Wiley City, she wished he'd come with her. His support would have been helpful. There was nothing that could be done for her Ma that Doc wasn't already doing, but Frank standing next to her, being someone for her to lean on would have helped her greatly. One thing she could focus on that helped her was when this was over and she could go home. She felt selfish for thinking that way, but she knew that would be when she could process everything and be free to let her emotions overtake her when they wanted to.

Allie wasn't sure if Pa would be ready when the time came for her to leave. She knew Drew would never be ready. Allie would need to separate herself from here to be able to breathe again. She couldn't begin to heal until she was gone. Holding in her feelings, especially around Pa and Drew, was tiring, but she didn't know what else to do. There had never been a time before that she couldn't get through to Drew. She always found a way to put a smile back on his face. Now she didn't know if she would ever see him smile again.

With Pa withdrawing more each day, she wasn't sure if he had any kind of a plan for the future, let alone a solid one. That worried her. She wasn't sure she could handle making all the arrangements by herself after her Ma passed, nor figure out what was to happen to Drew.

Allie would have to talk with Frank before she could take him home with her. Maybe Pa had been planning to keep him here with him. Or maybe Pa was thinking of moving. Wiley

City was so welcoming and still had room to spare. He could move to be closer to her and Frank.

That would be work and she wasn't sure if he was up to doing that. Not knowing what he was thinking, or planning, meant she couldn't plan for herself. The future remained unknown and despite working hard to learn to lean on God and let Him lead her life, applying that was still a struggle. She hoped one day that would come easily, but for now it was a conscious effort she had to make daily.

CHAPTER 18

Frank was sore from the train ride. It felt good to stretch his legs on his walk to Allie's parent's farm. His parent's would have to wait to see him. Allie was first. He knew the path there by heart. He had walked it countless times growing up. He stepped through the door, not needing to knock anymore, Allie froze.

He opened his arms and Allie ran into them. They stayed that way for a while until he took his hands and cupped her face to look into her eyes welling with tears. He gave her a soft smile and released her. He noticed how tired she looked and saw by the dark circles under her eyes she wasn't getting much rest.

"What are you doing here?" She questioned gratefully, still surprised to see him.

"Allie, I'm so sorry I didn't come with you. I should have been here. You need me and I wasn't thinking clearly." He kissed her. "Come on."

Frank walked her through the door and around the side

of the house putting his hand on her back and gave her a gentle shove towards the creek. She looked back over her shoulder once, but didn't need much convincing to continue on. He watched her walk down the slope to the creek's edge. He longed to go with her, but knew she needed some alone time. He decided he would check on Ma first and then meet up with Allie at the creek.

Ma was a slight lump in the bed. She was always a thin woman, but the cancer ate so much of her that she looked tiny. Her breathing was ragged and sporadic. Death was upon her and he was thankful he arrived before it was too late. Why he didn't come with Allie he would never know. This is what was important... what mattered. His heart was trying to tell him, but his brain refused to listen until he made a devastatingly huge mistake. He could never go back and do that again, but from here forward he vowed to listen more to his heart than he did in the past.

Frank checked Ma over as she slept, doing everything he was sure Doc had done numerous times already. There was nothing he could do for her, but wait. For Allie there was much to be done. He left and headed to the creek. Allie was in the water in nothing but her undergarments. She was laying propped up with her head on a rock. It didn't look comfortable, but he didn't think she was feeling anything anyway. He sat on the edge and watched her for a while. When she shifted positions he quietly spoke.

"Hey sweetheart."

Allie sat up and turned towards him.

"Hi," her reply so soft it was almost unheard.

She stood and waded over to him and sat down beside him. Ever since they were little, they had a tradition involving a penny. Anytime she seemed to be deep in thought Frank would pull out a penny and give it to her for her thoughts. She would take it and share. Then he'd give her advice to help her out. The penny would then be handed back as payment for the words of wisdom.

Frank pulled out a penny, placed it on his palm, and held it out for her without saying anything this time. Allie looked at the penny and sighed. She fell against him letting him take her weight, the penny left in his hand. He put it away and wrapped her up in his arms. He held her until she pulled away first.

"Did you see Ma?" She asked, staring down at the water.

"I did."

"Pa is around here somewhere. He's keeping busy. Drew is probably in his room. He hasn't said more than two words to me since I tried to talk to him several days ago. I don't know if he fully understands. He knows Ma is dying, but he implied that it was because I was here. Something about me doing Ma's work so she didn't have anything to do."

Frank knew Allie needed him. He didn't realize that the others might as well.

"I'll find Pa and see if I can help him. I can try with Drew, but I'm afraid you were always the one who could get through to him."

"Thanks, and I know. I just don't know how to proceed

with him."

"Well, I'm here now. How about we proceed together?" He touched his forehead to hers.

Allie embraced him and let him help her to her feet. She dressed, and they made their way back to the house to deal with these issues head on together.

Frank started with Drew first. He didn't think he'd get very far with him, but he would try. Drew was in his room right where Allie said he spent most of his hours these days. He was standing looking out the window. Frank stood next to him, but Drew wouldn't even acknowledge that he was there.

"Hi, Drew. How are you? Do you need anything?"

He might as well have been talking to a statue. Frank stood there and looked out the window as well. He could see Pa out by the barn. He was getting nowhere with Drew. Hopefully talking with Pa would be more successful.

Frank checked in on Allie before he headed outside. She was washing up some dishes and putting names on little pieces of paper to go with them. That way they could be returned to the rightful owners the next time she saw them. He knew people were only trying to be helpful. Sometimes being helpful meant making more work for the person. He left her there and went to find Pa. Afterwards, he would be back working side by side with her.

Pa was beside the barn. He was fiddling with the plow. It looked like he had hit a rock or something hard at some point. There was a dent in the metal blade.

"Hi, Pa."

"Frank! Well, hello. How are you doing?" He shook his hand and gave a hug with a pat on the back with his free hand.

"I'm doing all right." Frank pointed down at the blade. "You hit a rock?"

Pa tugged on his beard.

"Sure did. I was plowing a new field. Already put in the rest, but thought I'd break some more ground. Open it up and plow a few times this year. Get started for next year's planting."

Frank hesitated wondering why he wanted to plow up more land.

"Do you need more field to plant?"

Pa chuckled.

"Well, son, a farmer always expands. Have to keep growing."

"Sir, I understand generally yes, but do YOU." Frank looked directly at him with his eyebrows up. "Need more field?"

Pa sighed.

"I don't mean to upset you, Pa, but your family might be needing more time than your fields right now."

Pa turned his back on Frank and sniffed.

"Frank, I'm doing the best I can right now. Okay?"

It wasn't a question. Frank knew that. It was a warning.

All it did was anger Frank. It wasn't okay. It would never be okay. He'd hurt Allie enough as it was. She didn't need this from her Pa, too. Drew needed him. Ma needed him. He needed to pull himself together and act like the head of this household like he normally did.

Frank told Pa just that and waited for the heated return he expected. Instead he got silence. Pa's shoulders were shaking. Pa was crying. Frank stood still and let him cry for a bit. He suspected this might be the first time he was letting himself feel. Or maybe he was staying outside away from everyone, so he could do this in private.

"Pa?" He placed his hand on his shoulder. "They need you. Especially Drew. Allie is strong. She'll get through this and I'll be right there to help her in every way I can. Ma is at the stage where she doesn't really know what's going on anymore. But Drew, he's not ok."

"I know that!" He yelled out and turned to Frank. "I don't know what to do for Drew. I'm at a loss."

Frank could understand that. It was hard to know what was running through Drew's head when all was well. He was a mystery to him.

"Maybe if he saw feelings. If you just showed him how to work through all this. I think he's confused, scared maybe. He needs to be taught how to deal with his confusion. Just being there with him might be all he needs."

Pa thought about that a bit.

"It's just so hard, but maybe I'll give it a shot and see if it helps."

"Sure. And I'll talk with Doc. If Drew gets out of control once he starts letting his emotions run I'll have something ready to help calm him down."

Frank didn't like having to take that precaution, but Drew was a grown man with a child's mind. He could cause some serious damage if he wanted to.

"Thanks, Frank. Thanks for coming. Being here. This is harder than anything I've done. I always knew it would be hard when one of us went. When you've been with someone most of your life and then suddenly they are gone, you are at a loss for how to continue moving on. I didn't know just how hard though. No one can really know until it's staring you down."

"No problem, sir. I'm sorry all this is happening, but glad I ended up coming. Sorry it took so long."

Frank wrapped his arm over Pa's shoulder and together they walked back to the house. Pa's first step forward was talking to Drew. Frank returned to help Allie.

CHAPTER 19

Allie hadn't realized just how tired she was until Frank showed up. She felt like she could breathe again. Getting to spend some time at the creek nourished her soul. After Frank came in from talking with Pa, he kicked her out of the kitchen and sent her to bed. She protested at first of course, but knew he was right. She hadn't slept well since she'd arrived. There was just too much to do.

Frank was plenty capable of handling all the house stuff and he could take better care of Ma than she could, so she conceded and went to bed. When she awakened, she realized she had slept all afternoon and it was the next day. Even with knowing how tired she was, that had still surprised her.

Ma hadn't changed. She was holding steady in a deep sleep. All but Drew were taking their turn sitting and talking with her. Having a one-sided conversation was tough, so Allie usually either talked about past memories or read to Ma. Sometimes it seemed her breaths would strengthen with stories of the family's good times. No one knew if she could hear them, but Frank encouraged them to continue. Doc Leman stopped by and agreed with Frank. The two of them caught up briefly before Doc headed to another house call.

Allie hated seeing her ma in this stage and wished she would go. The wait was like standing at the station, not knowing if or when your train was coming. It would be easier when it was over for Ma and everyone else. Allie knew for certain her ma wasn't in any pain. She had even told her Ma that it was fine. That she could go and yet she didn't. She wasn't sure if she was waiting for something or if this was all involuntary.

Pa had spent time with Drew. He started by meeting him where he was up in his room. It was slow going, but after a while he was able to get him to play cards with him. After a couple of days Drew ventured outside and helped Pa in the fields.

Frank was concerned they were hiding out again, but Pa assured them that he was using the time to talk with Drew while he was able to hear him but have something physical to focus on as well. It helped him process everything. That was a big relief for Allie. She still wasn't sure what to do where Drew was concerned.

Pa walked through the door and headed into their room where Ma lay sleeping. He had been coming in more often and spending time with her. Allie was thankful for that and for the one who made all that happen. Frank was a big help to all.

Allie was sitting at the table working on a puzzle. Frank's parents had stopped in to see how things were going and brought the puzzle and a few other gifts. With Frank around her chore list was drastically reduced. He wouldn't let her do too much. Instead he was handling all of the work and, while Allie appreciated what he was trying to do, she was needing to do something useful to feel like she was helping Ma.

The puzzle would suffice for now as a distraction, but she would need to talk to Frank soon if he didn't let up on her restrictions some. Doing things helped her get through each day, and when she wasn't doing anything, all she felt was numb. She was in a limbo of waiting for grief. She had spurts of it here and there, but with Ma still hanging on, she wouldn't let herself dive fully into it.

"Frank, will you come in here? I need to speak to both you and Allie."

Pa made his way from his room and to the table where Allie sat. They all took seats and Allie laid her puzzle piece down she had been working on.

"Now, first I need to apologize. I know I wasn't much help to you Allie and I'm sorry about that."

"It's fine, Pa. I under..."

Pa held his hand up and she stopped.

"It's not. I am your father and I have neglected those responsibilities."

Allie and Frank glanced at each other before looking back at Pa postured straight as a plank, shoulders back and steady.

"Now, I should have talked all of this over with your mother while I had the chance. I thought that would make everything final then if I did. That I had lost hope. I see now that it wouldn't have mattered. The end result will still be the end result regardless of what I did."

Allie reached her hand across the table and placed it on top of Pa's. She remained silent waiting for him to share all he wanted. Pa looked to give into the gesture and softened a bit.

He paused and took a deep breath.

"Now, I have wasted that opportunity and must make decisions fully on my own. I have decided that since it was always our joint decision to keep Drew with us and not place him in Warm Springs mental facility, he will remain with me. It will not be easy. I know that. I think it would be best for him to stay here in the only home he has ever known. He has a long way to go in understanding how his future will change but removing him from his surroundings would make it worse."

Allie released a breath. She was prepared to speak with Frank about taking him, but now she wouldn't have to.

"And Pa, I want you to know that should things change, and you are struggling," she looked at Frank before continuing. "And as long as Frank is fine with it as well, you are both welcome to come to Wiley City."

Frank nodded in agreement.

"Thank you, both, but I'm hoping we can work into a routine here and won't need to move. Of course, when it's my time to go," he coughed. "Other arrangements will need to be made."

"We will cross that bridge when it comes. Let's get

through this first," Frank stated.

"I always thought I'd be going first. Life has funny ways of changing your plans. It all happens in His time, not in ours." Pa stood and scooted his chair in. "I'm going to go back in and let your Ma know I had this conversation. She would like to know we have a plan. Then I'll head back out to Drew.

At the same time, Drew walked through the door and headed to Ma's room. Pa followed him and Allie could hear them talking outside her door.

"Pa, I'm going in. I want to talk to Ma. You stay here." He pointed his finger in Pa's chest, turned and walked through the door, closing it in Pa's face.

"Well, I guess I'll just be hanging out right here then," Pa shrugged to Allie and Frank.

Drew hadn't been in to talk with Ma since Allie arrived. She wasn't sure if he did before then. What he wanted to say to her no one knew, but Pa was standing close to try and hear.

Drew wasn't in long and didn't stop to say anything to any of them before heading back outside. Allie did see the tear marks trailing down his cheeks before he slipped out. Pa went in to check on Ma. He was in there for a short time as Frank and Allie worked on the puzzle together really not sure what they should be doing.

"FRANK!" Pa shouted from the room.

Frank went running. Allie was hesitant to follow, but trailed after slowly. She stopped in the doorway.

"I was just talking to her. I told her my decision with Drew and after that she made a ragged breath and stopped."

Frank walked to the edge of the bed and checked her over. Frank looked into Allie's eyes and then to Pa's for what needed no words. She was gone. He normally would just say that it was finished, they are gone, or something to that nature, but he found it hard to speak. He took the sheet and covered her head instead.

Pa just stood there and stared, a blank stare his mouth slightly open. Allie crumbled to the floor sobbing. Frank moved to Allie and met her where she was.

"She was just here and now gone. Why now?" Pa laid down next to her. He pulled the sheet back down and was stroking her hair. I just, I wanted to tell her more." Pa buried his face in the sheets muffling his wavering voice.

Frank remained with Allie, holding her tight as she sobbed in his arms.

"She was going to go at any time. Maybe she was waiting for Drew to come in and say goodbye. Maybe she was waiting for you to reassure her you have a plan. Maybe it was just time. Maybe she put it in God's hands today."

They stayed that way for a few minutes before Pa got up realizing he needed to find Drew. He had a responsibility and he was going to see it through for his family. Drew needed to be told. He wasn't sure how Drew would respond, but he was ready to face it head on.

Pa found him in the barn. He didn't know exactly how to tell him, so he just said it. Drew looked at him for a while standing still before speaking.

"Okay, thanks."

Pa was stunned.

Okay, thanks? What did that mean?

"Drew, I'm not sure you understand."

"Yes, I do. I'm not stupid. Ma's body is dead. She's up in heaven now, though, waiting for us. It's okay. I thanked her for being a great Ma to me, told her goodbye, and gave her a hug and kiss."

"Oh, Drew," Pa wrapped him in a hug.

He still wasn't sure if Drew completely understood that being gone meant she wouldn't come back, but he wasn't going to keep pressing him now. He would take this as it was and they would move on. Somehow.

CHAPTER 20

Ma's funeral at their family church was standing room only. Allie sat in the front row instead of in their usual family pew. She was sandwiched between Drew and Frank. Pa sat on the other side of Drew, ready to react if need be. Drew behaved, though. He seemed to be taking all this the best out of the three of them.

Mr. Shirley, their pastor, stood at the head of the church in his best suit. Allie was sure he was giving a deep and meaningful eulogy, but she wasn't able to focus on his words. Her eyes stared straight ahead at her Ma's coffin that laid just beyond the pastor.

A nice floral arrangement was made and draped across it. Frank's parents provided that. They were sitting on the other side of Frank. Blinne, George, and Lena were directly behind. Allie had all of her people surrounding her. All but Ma. She knew she had to move on with life. Tomorrow would come, just like it always had, and somehow, she had to figure out how to move forward. She was tired, a deep exhaustion she had never felt before.

The whole congregation and other town's people who did not regularly attend this church were all in silent prayer before the pastor said his concluding remarks. People started making their way out of the packed church and into the yard where the women had pulled together a potluck.

They did this regularly, and Allie and her Ma took turns manning the tables. Allie wouldn't be asked to do anything today. None of her family would be and neither would Blinne. Everyone knew they were more like sisters and she was mourning as well.

Allie stayed seated in the pew with Frank by her side. Pa and Drew had gone somewhere, Allie wasn't sure where. Many people made their way to her. She remained sitting. She could hear the condolences as each person approached and she wanted to be nice and respond, but she couldn't. Her mind wouldn't let her body react. She sat frozen staring at the coffin. It was finished. After people were done eating they would leave and go about their business as though it was just another day.

Frank placed his hand on Allie's shoulder to get her attention. Then he used that hand to gently lift her under her arm and held her hand with his other. She rose and together in silence they walked out to the potluck. She wouldn't eat. She wanted nothing to do with any of this. She knew though as the daughter of the woman being laid to rest today, she was obligated to at least be present.

Blinne had dished a small plate for her. She knew Allie wouldn't eat, so she gave her just a little to nibble on. She sat next to Blinne, who was feeding Lena small pieces of cut up fruit. Juice was running down her face and she was squealing with delight at the yummy treat, eager for more. Blinne was feeding her as fast as she could while making sure Lena wasn't going to choke. Lena gave Allie a reason to smile and another reason to be sad. She needed to focus on something other than all this sadness.

Frank sat down next to Allie, his plate full. She glared at him, but quickly softened her features. She didn't want to be upset with him. He was doing everything for her. She didn't know how he could eat, though. She would rather throw up than eat.

"You really should try and eat, Allie," Frank said between bites.

Allie glared at him in full now, not concerned about being upset with him. Didn't he understand? She stood and quickly walked through the crowd, brushing against a few people as she moved through and away from everyone. A few people tried to stop her, but she shook free of them and continued on. Frank trailed behind her, but waited to stop her until they were away from the crowd out of earshot.

"Allie, wait." They kept moving on at the same pace. "Allie, stop!"

Allie stopped, but kept her back facing Frank. Frank grabbed her shoulder and gently spun her around. She had tears streaking down her cheeks.

"Oh Allie, come here sweetheart."

Frank tried to hug her, but she pushed him off and ran. Where she was running she didn't know. She just ran. Frank turned and saw that everyone was staring. They were far enough away they couldn't hear, but they could still see. Frank had decided to follow her instead of going back to the potluck when Drew approached.

"Frank, what did you say to her?" He crossed his arms.

"Drew, she's upset. I could have said anything and she still would be upset. She was very close to your Ma. It's going to take her some time."

"I know that. I'm not stupid, Frank. I know I'm slow. I know I take a while to know things. I know I wasn't always this way. I know Allie is hurting and I know why. You stay. I will go find her." Drew left Frank standing there and pursued his sister.

Pa broke away from the crowd and towards Frank.

"What's going on Frank?"

"Allie is upset. All I did was tell her she would need to eat sometime. I worry about her. Drew decided he needed to go find her."

Pa took a deep breath.

"You go back to the potluck. Reassure everyone that everything is fine. Your parents and George and Blinne can help you. I will follow, but I'm going to let Drew talk to her. Those two always have had a special bond. Maybe he can calm her down. Maybe this is good for both of them"

Frank reluctantly made his way back to the church yard. He quickly spoke to his parents and Blinne. They, of course, agreed to tell people that everyone was fine. Allie just needed some air and she would be fine was the story they agreed to. The story moved around, but it was evident that several didn't believe it.

She just lost her mother. She was entitled to an emotional outburst. He would protect her from here and let her be while making sure no one tried to follow. Frank ached to be by her side.

Allie kept running. She wasn't sure where she was headed. Her body took over. Before too long she found herself at her creek behind her parents' house. She tried to take a deep breath, but her lungs refused to fill. She fell to the ground and sobbed. She stayed that way for several minutes before she realized someone was there. Lifting her head and wiping her eyes to clear the blurriness the tears created, she realized Drew was watching her. She tried to speak to him, but all that came out was a wail. He crouched down next to her and held her while she cried more.

"Shhh, Shhh," Drew repeated as he was patting her head. Allie was beginning to calm down.

"I'm ok, Drew. I'll be okay," she said through hiccups.

"It's all right to feel sad, Allie. I'm sad, too."

Allie wiped her tears with the sleeves of her dress,

"Yes, it is, Drew. I'm sorry you're sad."

She wished she could have a deep conversation with him again, like the ones before the horse accident damaged his mind. She missed her brother.

"Ma's in heaven now. Pastor says that. He also says if I'm good I'll go to heaven, too. That means I'll be back with Ma. I will see her again and you can, too." Drew stated proudly.

"You're right about that." Allie thought for a minute. "How did you find me?"

"That's easy. This is where you go. This is your spot." They both chuckled, Allie's was a sad chuckle compared to Drew's.

She stood and realized Pa was standing in the distance. Drew looked back to see what Allie was looking at and saw Pa, too. He walked over to them

"Hi," He stood a couple feet away.

"Oh, Pa, I'm sorry I left." Allie felt a little embarrassed at the scene she must have caused.

"No need to apologize. It's understandable." Pa took both of his kids in his embrace.

"If you're ready, we should probably walk back. We left a lot of people there and Ma."

Allie's jaw dropped. "Oh no. I didn't think."

"Your Ma will wait for us. I'm sure about that. We do need to get her in the ground though." Pa was putting on a brave face, but inside saying those words crushed him. "Pastor Shirley is ready when we are for that part."

The second part of the day would begin when most of the town's folks left as this part was to be more intimate, just for close friends and family. They would move the coffin to the burial site where the hole had already been dug. Pastor would say a few more words and they would have one last goodbye before covering her up. That was the part Allie dreaded the most.

The three of them made their way back to find that many had already left. It seemed that Allie taking off was a cue for others to do the same. Frank met Allie and walked her the rest of the way. She gave him an apologetic look and he smiled softly back. She wasn't sure what she did to deserve this man, but she sure was thankful for him.

They moved through the next steps with Frank glued to Allie's side. She found herself sitting in a chair in the grass with a hole in front of her. Somehow her Ma had been moved and she vaguely remembered George, Drew, Frank, and a couple of other men carrying her out of the church.

Some moments of the day stuck out at her and slapped her across the face. Other moments seemed to move by without her paying attention. Pastor was saying a few words and read from the Bible, but his words seemed muted in her fog.

Pa stood and walked to the hole. He bent down and dropped his flower in. Drew followed and did the same. It was Allie's turn next. She didn't want to go. Going meant it was over.

Frank stood her up and her feet were moving beneath her. Before she realized it she was standing staring down in the hole. The coffin was there. Two flowers, red and white roses, were laying in odd angles on top. Frank was holding a flower, her yellow rose. Pa chose red to represent their love. Drew liked the white one. It was clean and Ma liked things clean. Allie chose the yellow that matched her Ma's bedroom curtains and the ones she made for her home. Yellow. The color that brought a bit of happiness to both Allie and her Ma.

Frank reached out for her to take it, but she refused. He tried one more time to hand it to her before he decided to drop it in for her. Then there were three flowers representing the three still living. All laying on top of the coffin in various positions.

Allie was reminded that she should thank Mrs. Wimble for providing the roses from her garden. It was a kind gesture and showed a side of her that many never saw. She did have a good heart down in there somewhere.

Allie smiled sadly and looked at Frank signaling them to move back to the seats. After Allie sat, a couple of the men that carried her Ma stood and began shoveling dirt atop the coffin, slow at first then with purpose. A tear slipped down Allie's cheek with each shovel of dirt that fell. She tried to focus on her breathing to keep it under control. Frank squeezed her hand and scooted closer.

She sat for a little while watching, but couldn't anymore. She stood, looked at Frank, Pa, and Drew. Then she scanned the other faces. Placing a fist covering her mouth and holding her other hand out to stop anyone that might try to stop her she made her second exit of the day.

This time she walked, she didn't run. She was in control but needed air. She needed to breathe and be alone. No one stopped her. They all understood and knew she would be ok. After Allie left, the others slowly made their exit after saying final words to Pa and Drew. Frank stood with them. His parents stood next to him for a while before they too left. They were the last three, except for those shoveling, watching the dirt fall.

"Frank, will you and Drew head back home. I'm going to stay here for a while longer." Pa kept his gaze focused on the dirt.

Frank knew Pa meant for him to take Drew home. He knew Pa wanted to be alone.

"Come on, Drew. Let's go home and see if we can do anything so there is less work for Pa and Allie.

"All right. Bye, Pa." Drew gave Pa a hug and with Frank headed for home.

Pa remained until the grave was fully covered. The men shoveling left, and he was all alone. He wasn't sure how he was going to move on, he just knew he had to.

The one he worried about before was fine. Allie was the one he needed to worry about. He would deal with his grief later. She needed him. He said a little prayer for Ma, for himself, for his kids, and asked for help. His faith was always strong. He needed to lean on that now to get him through. He walked slowly home.

Leaving his love buried in the ground was the hardest thing he'd ever done. If he could stay right there forever, he would, but he had living people who needed him. Yes, Ma was in God's hands now. It was His will and in His time to take her whether Pa wanted it or not. He needed God to carry him through this. He prayed the entire way home.

CHAPTER 21

The days blurred together. Without having to take care of Ma, Allie had more time on her hands. She used that to either sit at the creek or just wander around. She did that for several days before she realized Frank was waiting for her.

He didn't say anything, and he wouldn't. He was patient and knew she needed some time, but he needed to get back to Wiley City and his practice. But he wouldn't leave without her.

Allie needed to help Pa go through Ma's things before she could leave. She wasn't ready to do that. She wouldn't ever be ready. Today was the day they would need to tackle that job. She would tell Frank they could leave as early as tomorrow, if a train was available.

She found Frank in the kitchen with Drew. She stood silently in the doorway and watched for a minute. Even though their backs were turned toward her, she could hear their conversation.

"Now, Drew, you are going to want to add those eggs to

this flour and stir them in with the wooden spoon. Be careful not to get any shell in there."

"I know. I'll be careful."

Drew picked up an egg and was tapping it on the side of the bowl softer than needed. The egg wouldn't crack unless he used a little more force. Frank encouraged him to whack it a little harder. He did, and the egg broke in two.

Allie tried not to laugh out loud. She really did, but she couldn't help it. It just came out and both guys turned towards her. Frank smiled trying to control his own chuckle. Drew was scowling at her. Which made Allie shut her mouth, but she was still having troubles stopping the laugh all together.

"Oh, I'm sorry, Drew. It's funny, though."

"No, it's not. I need to learn and it's hard." Drew stated, turning back and trying another egg.

Frank walked to her and kissed her cheek.

"Your smile is lovely. I've missed it"

"So is yours. What are you two doing?" Allie inquired as she leaned to see Drew past Franks head, inadvertently dodging her husband's attempt for a kiss.

Drew growled as another egg shattered and Allie's smile grew.

"I'm teaching. Drew approached me the other day. Since it's just Pa and him, he decided he needed to learn how to do some more to help out. Today I'm teaching him all about biscuits. Well, technically we are stuck on the egg portion, but the goal is to get to the actual biscuit part... soon." He winked at her and tried once more for that kiss and again missed his mark as Allie turned towards Drew.

Allie's eyebrows raised.

"Wow, you are amazing Frank. Thank you."

"Just being a brother to him. He is capable of learning smaller things. It's good for him."

"Ma did teach him how to crack eggs, before the accident. He used to be fairly good in the kitchen, but he has forgotten, after, she stopped working with him on things like that."

Allie kept her words quiet. Then she realized that was the first time she said Ma without tears forming.

"Ah," Frank nodded his head. Drew broke the third egg and hit the counter. "I better get back over there."

Allie left them to their work and went in search of Pa. It didn't take long as he was in the barn brushing down one of the horses. He saw her, nodded once, and went back to work. Allie grabbed another brush and went to work with him. They stayed in silence for a moment before Allie broke it.

"I think it's time, Pa."

Pa didn't need an explanation of that. He knew what needed done.

"I reckon you're right."

Pa had avoided the room as much as possible, staying

up late and going in to sleep after dark. Then he would wake before daylight and leave. His eyes were tired and bags had formed below them. Allie wasn't sure if he was sleeping at all when he was in there.

"I've been thinking about what to do with her things. Most of her clothes could be donated to the woman's quilting club. Ma spent many hours quilting blankets for people around these parts. Those clothes could be pulled apart and turned into more quilts. She could still be doing her work in a way."

Pa cleared his throat.

"That is a wonderful idea. I think she would be very happy with that," he paused his brushing, lost in thought. "You should go through her other things first and see what you would like to keep. You can pick something out for Drew as well. I'm sure he would appreciate having something of hers."

"Of course," Allie agreed as she put away the brush. "Would you like to help me?"

"Not just yet. I'm going to finish up out here first. Let me know when you have all of her clothes taken care of. Then you can pull the other things out onto the table and I'll look them over before deciding what to do with them all."

Allie put her hand on Pa's arm.

"Sure. I will let you know as soon as that's done," Allie softly agreed and kissed his cheek, squeezed his arm, and headed to work.

Opening the door to her parents' room, Allie could slightly smell the remainder of death, although it wasn't as strong as it was in the days leading up to the passing. She walked to the window, tugged the cheery yellow curtains to the sides and opened it to let some fresh air in. She stood looking out the window, breathing the fresher air and tried to prepare herself for the task ahead. She decided she would lay the clothes out on the bed. Once they were all laid out she would see if Frank would take them to Mrs. Wimble for her. Allie wasn't ready yet to socialize, but she knew Mrs. Wimble would be more than happy to take them to the group for her. She went drawer by drawer pulling out all of the clothes. The undergarments would not go to the quilting group. Mrs. Wimble may know if they could be used by any of the local women. She tucked that thought back to mention to Frank when he drove them in.

Once those drawers were finished, she moved to collect the little trinkets and such. Ma had a bottle of perfume that she only occasionally wore, a small jewelry box with a few pieces in it including a brooch from her mother, a couple of hair pins, and her gold band that Pa placed there, her hair brush and hand mirror totaled everything that was on the dresser.

Allie bent down and pulled out the items from under the bed. There Ma kept a few items from Allie's childhood, a small doll and some wooden blocks Pa had made. Both Allie's and Drew's baby blankets were tucked under there, too.

Ma had made both while she carried them. In the middle was a square of needlepoint that depicted the season in which the baby was to be born. Allie's was white and green and Drew's was white and yellow, although the whites had become a dingy yellow color. The blankets were small and folded together. When Allie unfolded them a handful of needlepoint

136

squares fell out. Each one with a picture of a season. That confused Allie.

Those must have been made up ahead of time to make more blankets when needed. Perhaps they were for her future grandchildren.

Allie knew her parents dreamed of more children, but that wasn't in God's plan for them. They were happy with the two they had, or so they'd said. She briefly thought of including those with the clothing, but decided to wait until she could speak with Pa.

She carried everything out in two trips. From there, she explained to Frank her plan with the clothes and he agreed to hitch the team and drive them in today. Then she called for Pa to come in and go over everything with her.

Standing before the items as she waited for Pa she felt sad. Those few items were all that was left of her Ma. Of course, the dishes, cookware, blankets, towels, etc. were all a part of her, too. Those would remain here. Pa needed all of that to run the house. One day all of that would need sorted, but for now, just these few items were to be taken care of.

Pa walked in a bit reluctantly at first, and then changed to a determined get-in-and-get-done attitude. He scanned the table and turned to Allie.

"Have you decided what you might like to keep?"

"I have. I would like my baby things and I think Drew might like his. I would also love to have her brooch if that's all right with you."

Pa didn't speak for a couple of minutes thinking things over.

"That sounds fine. Ask Drew if he wants anything else. I will take her band and keep that."

"Pa, I found something I haven't seen before. I was wondering if you could tell me what they are and what I should do with them." Allie pulled the squares out from under her blanket.

Pa began rubbing his beard.

"Well now, uh, your Ma made those to speed the blanket making up when needed. The needlepoint part took more time than the quilt part. She had more time before you and Drew were born. She knew that'd be the case and made those all up beforehand. Yours and Drew's were made before, too."

"Oh. These are beautiful. Would you mind if I take them to use in case I ever have the need?" Allie's voice caught and she cleared it. Pa knew the story and knew the chances were stacked against them, but hope remained.

Pa pulled his little girl in for a much-needed hug.

"I think she would love that. It would be a way she could give a part of her to her grandchildren."

"Pa, we know there might not be any. I have to keep telling myself that."

He released the hug and looked into her eyes.

"God can work miracles, Allie. Don't lose hope. If a

family is what you're supposed to have it will happen."

Allie nodded and blinked several times to clear her eyes. Pa grabbed her chin and gave it a squeeze while scrunching his nose at her. She smiled back at him.

"Go ahead and see what Drew might want. I'm fine with all of this. He headed back outdoors and Allie forged ahead with finishing the task at hand. She would tell them all during supper that she was ready to head for home.

Pa seemed sad, but she knew he would get through this. Having Drew gave him something to do and reason to continue on. If they had placed Drew in the home like everyone wanted them to do after the accident, the situation may have been different. She was always glad they chose to have him remain home. She had an added reason for that now.

CHAPTER 22

In reality only a handful of weeks had past, but Allie felt as though months had gone by. Allie was worn out. She didn't want to leave Pa and Drew but knew she must head home with Frank.

Blinne came by to spend the last little bit with her, which she was grateful for. Allie had been working to make sure Pa was stocked up with bread and with a few meals put together as well as getting all of the chores for the week done. His work load would greatly increase when she left. Blinne was helping her with the last of it all.

"I'll take these blankets in from the line and get the beds made up," Blinne said, pulling them off the clothes line. She carried them into the house leaving Allie tending to the neglected garden.

Ma and Pa had been able to get it in together and Pa kept it watered, but with everything going on, the weeds were not a priority. They were putting in a fair attempt at taking over space. Pa would need this food to put up for the winter. If there were only weeds, they would be mighty hungry.

Frank headed to town to say his goodbyes to his family and Doc. He also needed to purchase their fare for the train. Later he would be back and would also pitch in and help with the last minute chores.

Company had slowed now that Ma passed. What was once a revolving front door of friends, neighbors, and community members turned into a wooden shield that very few tried to penetrate. She supposed they were just giving her family some grieving space, but the quiet only added to drawing out the length of the day.

Going home to Wiley City would be a nice break. Moving about and doing daily activities without anyone giving her looks of pity or empty words of condolences would be a breath of fresh air.

Allie didn't need anyone's help in making her feel horrible, she did that all on her own. She deeply missed her ma and knew the hole that formed when she passed would get bigger before it could start to heal. She couldn't help thinking about herself though. Losing her ma wasn't the real creator of the empty space within her. It just opened it up more. She had been feeling empty for too long to count now.

"Hello, sweetie. How's my wonderful wife doing?"

Oh, how she loved that voice!

Allie looked up and blocked the sun that was brightly shining in her eyes to see Frank standing before her. He was smiling and offering her his hand. She took it and pulled herself up.

"I'm all right. How are your parents?"

He wrapped her in a hug and kissed her temple.

"They're great. Both will miss us, though. They enjoy having us in town, but understand that we need to get back. I was able to see Doc for a bit. Glad, too. I picked his brain on typhoid. We have to figure out where it's coming from. Everyone knows water, but that could still mean any number of things. Doc gave me some information on treating it and things I should investigate. Boiling the water, he agrees, is the best approach for prevention at least until we know how it's spreading." Frank bent down and began where Allie had left off with the weeds.

"I would like that figured out soon, too. I'm not really sure I can deal with another death," Allie sighed.

"I understand that," Frank nodded. "Why don't you go in for a while? I'll finish up here."

"That I will do," she turned to leave and then looked back. "Were you able to get the tickets?"

"I did. We leave in the morning." Frank didn't look up, but kept working at the weeds.

Allie left Frank to get a drink of water and check on Blinne. She found her up in her old bedroom changing the sheets.

"Care for me to help?"

"That would make this go faster, I suppose," she smiled and handed a side of sheet to Allie and together they made short work of this bed.

"We're leaving in the morning. Frank was able to purchase our fare."

Blinne paused. She was going to miss Allie dearly. They would go back to corresponding, but it just wasn't the same.

"Sounds like after we finish, we should get you packed up."

Allie nodded. She and Frank had been staying in this room. Repacking her trunk would take little work. She hadn't brought much along, three dresses including the one she was wearing, undergarments, her apron, and a few toiletries. Her trunk was packed in a matter of minutes.

"Allie, I have something for you. Wait right here. I'll be back in just a moment."

Blinne headed downstairs and left Allie guessing what it could be. She hoped Blinne hadn't purchased anything for her.

When Blinne returned she had something hidden behind her back.

"One of the times I was here before, I was given something to hold on to and give to you after."

Allie was confused.

"Please just tell me. What is it?"

Blinne pulled a book from behind her back.

"I promise I haven't read it. It's private and meant for

your eyes only." Blinne reached the book towards Allie, her eyes fixed on it.

Allie hesitantly took the book and opened the cover. Tears ran down her cheeks and she reached out to hug Blinne.

"Oh! It's a journal. My Ma's journal. I didn't even know she had one."

"She had me keep it for you. I am curious to know what's in there, but I'll wait for you to share, if you feel like doing so."

"Of course, I'll share with you. I'm just so speechless and a little scared. Ma was always a closed book. She hinted at the possibility of things, but she would never tell me her history. Not all of it anyway. I of course know the story of how Ma and Pa met and married. I know about my grandparents. I'm sure that's in here, but maybe I might learn more." Allie hugged the book. "It feels almost like I have the opportunity to talk to Ma again. Thank you."

"Don't thank me. Thank her. I just did what she asked me to do," Blinne grasped her hands behind her back. Proud of her accomplishment of keeping a secret.

"I wonder why she just didn't give it to me herself."

"I don't really know, but maybe the answer is in there."

Allie hugged Blinne again. "Oh, thank you thank you thank you."

Blinne pulled back and set her jaw.

"Stop thanking me. It was nothing, really. Now, let's get

back to getting you ready to leave, shall we?"

Allie nodded, and again hugged the book. She still didn't want to go, but now she desperately wanted to read. Not knowing what this book, these pages held, made her want to read in private. She wasn't sure what or if she was going to learn anything, but she knew she wanted to know and absorb whatever was in here before anyone else knew.

With the book always in the front of her mind, the day passed much more quickly than any of the others. All of the chores were complete, thanks to having the extra hands to get it done. She couldn't always be here to help Pa, but at least she started him off right. She went to sleep in her bed for the last time with mixed feelings. She was sad to be leaving, again, but so anxious to go.

CHAPTER 23

Frank thought he was ready to go home and continue his practice, but the reality of what had happened bore down on him full force. He began doubting himself and his abilities before he stepped off the train in North Yakima. Refusing to let Allie see any turmoil within himself, he kept a smile on his face and worked to keep the conversation away from him or the practice.

They boarded the streetcar that serviced Wiley City, for the first time, and walked home from its stopping point. Frank carried their trunk. He was glad that it wasn't large and that they'd traveled light. As they turned the corner and their home came into view, they both stopped, not believing what was before them. Someone had built the fence! They not only built it, but painted it white as well. It didn't take Frank long to figure out John either did the work himself or organized it to be done.

"Frank! It's lovely," Allie commented, quickening her pace, making it home before her bewildered Frank.

When Frank caught up, he set down the trunk and

admired the fine work.

"This must have been John. I had picked up a load of wood and was going to build it for you myself... until..." Frank immediately stopped talking and turned his back to Allie.

Allie furrowed her brow.

"Until what?"

Frank ran his hand through his hair as he turned to face Allie.

"Uh, until I realized I should be with you. I dropped everything and came." He wrapped his arms around her. "I should have gone with you and I know I've apologized before, but I am sorry."

"Oh, Frank, stop. You did what you needed to. I'm happy that you did come, but I understand the pulls you have here." She headed for the door raising her voice for Frank to hear her as she walked away. "I'm going to bake something for John as a thank you. Need to see what I have to work with."

Frank picked up the trunk and followed her in the house. He took the trunk up to their room and set it at the foot of their bed. Then he went back down and found Allie was already busy in the kitchen. She had started a fire in the stove and had begun filling a pot with water to boil. Not much could be done until the water had boiled. He sat at the table and kept her talking so he didn't have to think about what truly was weighing on his conscience.

"How are you today? I know losing your Ma was hard, but you seem to be handling it better than I prepared for."

Allie paused and thought about what he just said.

"I'm ok, today. Right now. Honestly, it's like climbing a mountain. You go up a bit and then down some before going back up. The top is the goal, but you do have those downhill sections while climbing. I just hope once I get to the top nothing pushes me over and makes me fall down the other side."

Frank nodded. He could understand that. Losing Allie's Ma was the closest he has come to a death that directly affected him. His grandparents on his Pa's side died before he was born leaving the bank in his care. His mother's family lived back east and he didn't know them except through letters. He'd been around and witnessed many deaths, but more from an outsider's view. In many ways, this was the same. The only difference was that it affected Allie directly and that affected him. He didn't want Allie to hurt, but knew the grieving process took everyone a different amount of time. It looked different. Each person had their own path through the sorrow and moving on. He would be there and walk through it with her.

Frank decided to lighten the mood and change the subject while he watched Allie work.

"You sure make cooking attractive," he smirked.

"Frank! I'm head to toe in flour and sugar."

She had tied her hair back and knew her rosy cheeks and long eye lashes did always seem to bring something out in Frank. It didn't take too long and she had a plate of cookies put together. He wasn't really sure how she accomplished that, given the lack of supplies in their kitchen. She worked miracles, it seemed. Perhaps she was truly his angel.

"I'll walk this over now. I need to talk with him about what has gone on while we were away. I'm hoping not much, but tomorrow I will be opening up again and want to make sure I don't need to visit any patients for illness or injury that occurred in the last weeks." Frank dropped a kiss on her blushing cheeks and left her to clean up.

John wasn't too hard to find. He was the local blacksmith and his shop was by the livery. The smell of the hot steel seemed to overpower that of the stables, so Frank imagined John wasn't bothered by the location. Frank stood along the shop wall and waited for John to lift his head from his work and spot him.

"Well, hello Frank," John greeted, as he took his gloves off, wiped his brow, and walked over to pump his free hand.

Frank held up the plate of cookies. "Allie made these for you as a thank you. You did a fine job on that fence."

John smirked.

"No thanks necessary. I had help. Besides, that's what we do here. All pull together when someone needs something."

Frank nodded his reply.

"So, how is Allie's Ma?" John said still chewing and dropping crumbs from his lips.

Frank leaned against the wall once more and crossed one leg over the other.

"She passed a few days back."

John stopped his chewing and tried to clear his throat

for an apology. Frank lifted his hand and motioned it was ok.

"Losing someone is always hard, but losing family is tough. They are good folks and I think they will all be just fine."

"Glad to hear that, not the part about her passing, but about them being ok," John said and downed the last of the cookie.

"So, what has happened here while I was gone?" Frank closed his eyes. "How is the Dodd family?"

John wiped his mouth and brushed his hands off on his pants.

"They'll be all right, Frank. They lost both their parents and, as you know, it was a shock to them. That family is how you described Allie's, though. They are wading through their grief, but moving forward. The farm is for sale. All the kids have their own places, and most don't live around these parts anymore. It was the natural solution." John picked up the shoe he had been working on and looked it over before continuing. "It's a good farm. They'll have a buyer soon."

Frank silently thanked God. He hoped they were all doing well. Getting news that your father passed and rushing home to help your Ma only to have her die before your own eyes, could cause anyone to form demons that could eventually take them, too. That was not a chain reaction he wanted to be the start of.

"Thanks for letting me know they are managing alright."

John could see the pain flash across his eyes.

"I hope you aren't still blaming yourself. You know she would have done that anyway she could. A person gets that in their mind and it's hard to convince them otherwise. The way I see it, she took the easier to deal with approach. It could have been far worse on those kids of hers."

Frank's mind conjured up several horrible images. He was glad she didn't choose a more gruesome approach to taking her own life.

"It's a mistake I will always blame myself for. I became a doctor to save lives and to comfort those that were beyond saving. I never wanted any action of mine, accidental or not, to be the cause of someone's demise." He looked at his boots and tapped a small rock across the shop floor.

"It's over. What happened, happened, and that can't be changed. To be honest, it was an innocent mistake. I know if you could go back and take those pills away you would, but that can't happen."

John was sounding much like Allie's Pa in the matter of fact tone he had.

"Life moves on and those kids are going to be just fine." Frank nodded, but John could tell he was still wrestling with all of it. "I hope you can move on from this, and soon. We've had some issues crop up around here that need a focused doctor."

Those words snapped Frank to attention.

"What things?" Frank left his place on the wall.

"Typhoid."

One word was all that was needed. Everyone knew the area was plagued with it. The epidemic was on its third year and outside help had been requested.

"The number of deaths has increased lately. Wiley City itself has been affected. Just a couple of folks living out in the country. It hasn't directly hit the town, yet," John explained.

Frank knew this was a real possibility. He'd tried to get word out to as many folks as he could that they needed to use boiled water, but it seemed some just didn't believe that was a necessity. Maybe with the sudden increase in local cases it would catch their attention.

"Will you do me a favor, John?'

"Sure, what do you need?"

"Please help me spread the need to boil all water before it's used. All water for cooking and washing needs to first be boiled. That's the only prevention we have until we can figure out the source."

"Will do. We've been boiling since you told us, but I will make sure everyone I see understands the importance of it."

"Thanks, and thanks again for the fence. That brightened Allie's heart."

"Glad to do it."

They shook hands again and Frank headed for home with a long stride and a quick step.

CHAPTER 24

Allie had unpacked the trunk and pulled out the journal. She sat in the light of the bedroom window and began reading. She wanted to wait until she was alone. Somehow the yellow curtains alongside her made it seem as though Ma was right there. She had told Frank about the journal but he hadn't pressed her for more information, for which she was thankful. She would share later only what she wanted. Having this felt like she had a part of her ma still. She could keep it and hold the words in her heart as long as she wanted before releasing them.

She reclined on the bed and opened the cover. The front of the book had an elegant butterfly decorating the soft blue fabric that had some wear and soil splotching. Turning the first page, she saw her ma's name written in a beautiful script. It was printed. This book was made for her ma. Her parents never had much money for frivolous things. That made her curious as to how she obtained the book. Turning that page gave her the first answer. It read, *To our loving daughter, Doreen, on her sixteenth birthday. With all our love, Mother and Father.*

Allie gently rubbed the letters with her index finger. She

153

knew her grandparents were financially better off than her parents. Nothing was ever directly said, but Ma had a more refined upbringing and passed those skills off to her children.

Allie was taught things, such as how to set a table with multiple pieces of silverware or how to keep conversation light and upbeat in mixed company, things that other simple farm girls would not have learned. Life on the farm was busy with chores and learning necessities for survival. Ma found time to fit in these extra teachings here and there when time allowed.

Allie paused, thinking about Ma and Mrs. Wimble's relationship. Not many could be in Mrs. Wimble's company for very long. Ma seemed to know how to talk with her... what to say and when. She wondered if how Ma was raised had anything to do with that. Continuing on, she turned the page.

Allie recognized her ma's handwriting right away and it brought fresh tears to her eyes. She quickly cleared them, so she could see the first entry dated August eighteenth in the year of one thousand eight hundred eighty-two.

Mother and Father were very generous in giving me this journal. It is beautiful. My birthday party was held at my mother's place of work and where we live, the home of Mr. and Mrs. Richardson. Mother is their children's governess, and father serves as bookkeeper. It is rare that my mother stayed employed, having married and her own children, but the Richardson's are like family to us and allowed her to stay on. I have grown up next to their children, and mother has trained me the same.

That explained so much to Allie already and she was enjoying every little detail she learned. She continued reading.

The Richardson's are very generous people. They allowed us to use the garden outside. Camille, their chef, baked a lovely cake with little flowers on top for decoration. Tea was served to accompany the cake and I was allowed to invite several of my friends to the party. It was all very lovely, and I will forever cherish this day.

Mother says now that I am sixteen it is time for me to start thinking about my future. I didn't need persuading for that, though. I've been dreaming about that for a few years now. I am no longer a child, but a woman ready to spread my wings and fly, just like the butterfly on the front cover.

Mother has hopes that I will be fancied by one of the Richardson's children's friends. She would love for me to be wed off to an affluent member of society. I wish to fall in love and be swept away. Mother says those are wishful thoughts that rarely become reality, but I continue to hope. It is getting late and I must rest for tomorrow. We have to escort Helen, their oldest daughter, to town. Helen is slightly older than I and is preparing for her upcoming wedding. She will be meeting with the dressmaker for her final fitting. Mrs. Richardson has business to attend to at home. She fully trusts mother to handle this portion. Mrs. Richardson has already seen the dress a few times, and really this is just a formality of picking up the dress and brining it home. I will try to write again soon, but with the wedding approaching there is much to do and everyone must work together.

Allie closed the book just as she heard the front door latch. She rose and went downstairs to find Frank.

Frank hung his hat on the hook by the door and greeted Allie.

"Hello, darling. Did you miss me?" He winked.

"Yes, you have been gone for so long," Allie laughed. Frank had been gone an hour at most. "Did John enjoy the cookies?"

"He sure did. And, I was right. It was him... the fence work out there," Frank pointed to the front yard. "I don't know how we got so lucky, but the people around here are gems."

"That they are. And yes, we are lucky."

"You are still in a great mood."

Allie looked down at the floor remembering what she read.

"Yes, I'm learning about my Ma's history and so far, it's beautiful."

Frank sat in one of the chairs. "Ah, the journal."

"Yes, the journal," Allie joined him in the other chair. "She received it on her sixteenth birthday. So far I have only read the entry from that day. She had a wonderful party and I learned a bit more about my grandparents."

"That's great. I'm not sure why you didn't know this information before, but I'm glad she is telling you now, in her own words."

Allie sighed.

"I don't know either. She would give us bits and pieces. I knew she had a good childhood. I knew my grandparents were hard workers, but I didn't know details about that. In her own words is exactly how it feels. When I read, it felt as though she was right there telling me. I could hear her voice. I'm so happy I have this."

Tears pooled in her eyes and Frank reached over and grabbed her knee.

"I miss her," Allie confessed. She closed her eyes and raised her wrist to dab a tear.

"I know. It's okay. Cry when you need to cry. Laugh when you need to laugh. This is all part of this journey."

Frank decided a change of topic was needed.

"John told me that typhoid has been spreading since we left."

Allie wiped her eyes with her apron.

"Oh no! I was hoping things would improve. Is there something more I can do or should be doing?"

"No. Nothing. He said outside help is on its way. I'm going to reach out to Dr. Green in North Yakima and see if I can get any more information."

Allie chewed her lip.

"That sounds like a good idea. I really hope it doesn't get too bad. I don't know how much more my heart can take right now. I need life to settle down a bit. It seems things just jump from one thing to the next."

"I know what you mean. You've had over a year now with some pretty intense things to deal with." Frank's eyes twinkled just a bit. "You have had one big great thing happen, though."

Allie looked at him funny for a minute and then broke into a smile.

"Yes, I married the most wonderful, patient, giving man I have ever known." She moved from her chair and sat on his lap.

He pulled her in for a kiss.

"And, I married the most beautiful, generous, modest, lovable, responsible..."

Allie pushed his shoulder.

"Oh, stop." They both giggled and kissed some more.

CHAPTER 25

Frank and Allie headed in different directions for the day. Frank left early in the morning for North Yakima to meet with Dr. Green and learn more about the typhoid epidemic and specifically what his own role would be in this matter. Allie headed to her quilting group for the first time since returning from Montana. While Frank left feeling troubled about the puzzle ahead for the local medical community, Allie was feeling hopeful.

Reading her Ma's journal was bittersweet, and she could use a break to take her mind off everything related to the recent events. She knew Ma's passing was all part of God's timing, but she was unsure of where her own life fit into that plan.

The last couple of years had a few ups, but mostly downs. Frank was the biggest, brightest spot in her gloomy period. While that spot sparkled in the dark, the weight of what she'd been through felt too much to bare at times. Stepping into the cocoon of the woman's circle and letting her fingers work while her mind stayed busy in the comings and goings of the rest of the community was exactly what she needed.

Allie heard the laughter from the side room where they met each week as soon as she walked through the church doors. The sound brought a hopeful lightness to her heart and put a small smile on her face. She stepped into the room and the conversation stopped. Those that were there looked at her silently for the briefest of moments, but long enough for Allie to feel a bit nervous. Emma stood and walked over to her while Belle walked over to the stove in the corner.

"Oh, Allie, I'm so happy to see you. How are you?" Emma pulled back from the hug and looked her in the eyes.

"I'm all right. I'm doing okay," Allie said taking a deep breath. She really didn't want to talk about any of this and hoped she could just blend in and have time off from her grieving.

"Here, dear, have this cup of tea and come sit."

Belle handed her a tea cup and lead her to a chair. Belle and Emma sat on either side of her, sandwiching her between her two closest friends here in Wiley City. The other ladies took turns saying hello. Most of them held sorrow and pity in their eyes when they looked at her. She could feel her skin crawling and wanted to scream but chose to keep her manners.

Allie nodded and greeted each one. She answered their questions about her time in Montana. As the conversation drew on, Belle squeezed her hand and leaned into whisper in her ear.

"They only mean well dear."

Allie knew her tone was short and becoming shorter when answering and she looked at Belle with pleading eyes.

"Well now, ladies, it appears that most have arrived. Shall we hear about the newest quilt project we're to begin working on?" Belle had directed the whole table to follow her lead and change the conversation. Allie was immensely grateful.

The next hour became exactly what she was hopeful for and she had Belle to thank for that. The quilt they were working on was another design where some ladies would work on squares individually- those with embroidery skills and others would work to attach the plain fabric squares together into strips. Allie was part of this second group. Belle moved over with the first and Allie felt a small loss when she was distanced from her. She hadn't known Belle very long, but her presence was becoming important to her. Emma stayed right next to her. Allie took some comfort in that.

While the squares they were working on were plain, the color of those squares were bright. This blanket was to go to a new baby boy. It would be larger than a receiving blanket. This would be big enough for his mother to lay on the floor where the baby could play.

Each square Belle and the others worked on would show a different embroidered animal. Allie was excited about this project and couldn't wait to see it finished.

She knew she needed to move on, but the work made her a tad sad. Someday she hoped she would move on from her desire to be a mother and the reality of knowing that was a very bleak dream.

Grieving over her ma was enough for her right now. Grieving over the loss of nonexistent children and one lost precious little life was overwhelming. She tried to shove her thoughts to the side and focus on the task at hand, sewing one bright color to another after another until she had a strip of six squares. Those would make the outside edge with an animal square at either end. More animal squares would be positioned in the interior of the quilt as well. While Allie and Emma could work on their task weekly here, the others working on the embroidery would take their square home to continue working on it and thus not slow down the completion of the whole quilt.

Before Allie realized it, ladies were excusing themselves for the week. The hour they met had passed, and it was time to head for home. Emma walked out with her.

"Are you free tomorrow afternoon?"

"I believe so. Frank most likely will be working, leaving me to twiddle my thumbs," she smiled and worked to hide the sadness.

"Perfect. I will come see you. I have some news I would love to share with you."

Emma was practically glowing with excitement and Allie was curious. She could use some good news these days.

"I'm intrigued," Allie squinted her eyes.

"I'll see you tomorrow then," Emma chuckled as they parted.

When Allie entered her house, Frank was sitting in the living room. Allie was shocked to see him. She didn't expect him home for some time yet.

"Hello. How was North Yakima?"

Frank stood and walked towards her.

"The news isn't great, I'm afraid. It seems John was right. Many are sick and more are falling ill daily."

Allie covered her mouth in shock.

"Oh, Frank. I don't know how much more I can take. I'm sorry, but it's all so overwhelming."

"Of course, forgive me. I'll deal with it. I shouldn't burden you anyway. There isn't anything you can do to help that you are not already doing." Frank put his hand on the small of her back. "Please come sit."

"Suddenly, I'm so tired. I was feeling fine, but now I'm exhausted."

"You've been through so much lately. You barely slept the whole time you were taking care of Ma. It's no wonder you're tired. I want you to put this typhoid scare out of your mind. We have help coming in. Mr. Lumsden has been called to come assess the problem. He is a typhoid expert, and the hope is that he will be able to use his skills to understand and correct the issue."

Frank stood and helped Allie stand as well.

"Come, let's take you to bed for a nap." He led her to their bedroom where he settled her under the covers.

"I'll worry about supper. You rest. I'd say a week or two

of resting and focusing on yourself and you will be good as new."

Frank laid on the bed and waited until Allie fell asleep before going back downstairs. Inwardly kicking himself, he knew he shouldn't put any strain on her. She was already dealing with too much. Her care was the immediate focus. Up until this moment, typhoid had been an outside problem for him directly. He hoped it stayed that way, but until that changed, Allie would be his focus.

While he placed Allie in the forefront of his mind, typhoid would remain lurking in the background. Lumsden was their hope. Time was ticking and they needed to get to the bottom of this situation before it exploded beyond what it already had.

CHAPTER 26

Allie woke later that evening and Frank made her stay in bed. He brought her a light supper and she felt blessed. Frank doted on her. After her last husband, Frank was an angel. He joined her in bed with his supper and they talked about nothing. It was easy and peaceful.

She fell back asleep shortly after eating and slept through the night. The next morning she woke to a newfound energy. Resting was exactly what she had needed, and she was thankful the doctor ordered it.

She made her way downstairs and found Frank had already done the morning chores and had tea heated on the stove for her. She poured a cup and sat at the table giving herself a moment to fully awaken. As she did so, she remembered that today was not an ordinary day. Emma was to come this afternoon. Excitement grew within her and she thought about what she would need to do to prepare for her visit.

The house needed some freshening up. Dust had accumulated on all surfaces while they were in Montana. A baked treat to nibble on would also be in order, and she supposed she'd better change into proper day attire.

Allie set her tea cup down in search of Frank. If he wasn't with a patient, she wanted to say good morning before getting busy. She gently tapped on the door and waited. He wouldn't open it if someone was there. He did, however, open it wide greeting her with a smile and a good morning.

"How are you today?"

Allie paused and truly thought about her answer, before speaking.

"Today is a good day."

"Good! But, remember that emotions might spring up on you still," he cautioned.

Frank was concerned for her. Yet, a spark of optimism was noteworthy.

"Yes, and I will work some rest in today, but I do have a visitor coming. I forgot to mention it to you yesterday."

"Oh?"

"Emma is stopping by this afternoon. She says she has some news she would like to share with me, good news."

Frank was glad to hear the good part. He didn't want anyone upsetting her.

"Please, enjoy yourself, but don't overdo it."

"Yes, doctor," Allie winked and left him to his work, so she could do hers.

They hadn't yet accumulated many things making the dusting an easy chore. Since Frank converted the dining room, that left just two rooms and the entry. After dusting, she swept all the floors. That was a bigger chore than the dusting, as there was more floor than anything else.

Standing back up after collecting the swept dust into the dustpan, she briefly felt as if she would fall over. The room started to spin before righting itself again. She carefully walked over to the chair and sat for a moment, confused as to why she would feel this way. The tired was expected after Ma's death, but dizzy? Then a thought came to her that fit the puzzle piece together. She forgot to eat this morning, and with last night's light supper, she needed sustenance. The excitement for the day took all the hunger pains away.

Allie headed to the kitchen and found a bite to eat before beginning to think about what she would bake. Noting that she would need more food and Frank would need something for lunch soon, she decided on muffins. She had a basic recipe from her Ma that she could add different things in to change it up. There was some dried fruit that she could fold into the batter. She would need to add to the meal for lunch, but the muffins would be enough for her visit later.

Allie mentally doubled the batch and got to work. Making the simple recipe from her ma brought back fond memories of when she was a little girl and her Ma was teaching her. It was one of the first recipes she learned. This was the recipe she perfected her egg cracking skills on and that thought brought back the more recent memory of Frank teaching Drew.

That brought a full on laugh from her. As the laughter died down she began humming Crown After Cross a song she grew up hearing her ma sing. The words played in her head as the melody flowed from her throat. The song spoke about strength after weakness and joy after sorrow. She needed to take those words to heart. That was certainly something she'd hoped for but was yet to find.

As she finished mixing the batter and checking to make sure the stove was heated sufficiently, she placed the muffins in the oven and contemplated how the fire contained within the stove took something mushy and weak, and changed it so it could stand on its own instead of collapsing into a puddle.

That was how she felt her past year was to her. The fury within her marriage had prepared her to become a woman who could stand up for herself. No longer was she the young girl, but a strong woman who she felt was still being baked. Allie had thought the transformation from girl to woman was complete, but with the crushing death of her ma, she realized she still had a ways to go. She knew that God used life events to work for the good in all those around. She had grown up believing that. She wished that her ma didn't have to die, but everyone died at some point.

Pushing all thoughts aside, she ran upstairs to freshen up while lunch was baking. She wasn't sure on the exact time for Emma's visit and wanted to be ready. She picked out a summer dress, put a light pink ribbon in her hair and evaluated herself in the mirror. Coming back downstairs, she finished meal prep and let Frank know it was ready. He came in and washed up, all the time admiring his wife's attire. They sat together eating and Frank caught her up on his morning. Apparently, it was fairly busy. She hadn't heard the comings and goings being so distracted with her chores and thoughts.

Frank kept the conversation light. His morning was busy, but nothing serious happened. He looked Allie over to make sure she wasn't hiding anything. A person run down was more susceptible to catching a serious illness and he would do what he could to prevent that. She appeared to be fine, so he finished up and headed back to the office. If his morning was any indication of the full day, he would be there right up until closing.

Allie was cleaning up when Emma knocked on the door.

"Hello, I'm so glad you came! Please, come in."

Allie ushered her in and led her straight back to the kitchen, where they sat at the table. She placed the muffins in arms reach of them both. Just having eaten lunch, she wasn't hungry, but she could nibble a bit on one as Emma enjoyed hers.

"Hasn't the warm weather been lovely? I'm so thankful that winter is behind us and the sun can warm me clear through," Emma said between bites.

"It is lovely. The weather here isn't much different from what I'm use to in Deer Lodge," Allie replied. "You didn't come here to talk about the weather, though," Allie playfully glared at her. "Spill it."

Emma chuckled.

"No, I didn't, and I suppose making you wait after I teased you yesterday with news isn't very friendly of me, is it?"

"It sure isn't, and I feel you are still dragging this on for the fun of it."

Both ladies laughed. Emma cleared her throat.

"Our family will be growing by one in about seven months if my math is correct."

Allie sat frozen. She had been through this before and here it was again. She needed to show Emma she was happy for her and yet happy was not the emotion she was feeling. Emma and Roger had two children already. Now a third was to join. Life was not fair.

"Oh, Allie, I'm sorry. I didn't think you would find this news upsetting," Emma apologized, seeing Allie withdraw in thought.

Allie placed her hands in her lap.

"Oh, don't think of it. It is an exciting time for you and I am very happy for both you and Roger. Another baby to love, to hold, to teach. That is every good reason worth living right there."

"Is everything all right?" Emma worried her brows.

Allie was silent, thinking about how much she should say. She didn't want to share the horrid details with her, especially now. Emma was celebrating, and she had every right to do so.

"Everything is fine," she tried to sound as chipper as possible. "I do have a bit of a history that you don't know about. Someday I may share, but I'm not ready yet."

Emma didn't want to push her and tried to change the subject instead.

Allie however was lost in thought.

"I'm sorry, Emma. I suddenly feel very tired. Frank told me to rest when this happens. He said it's all due to the recent events."

"Of course. I had plans to stop in and have Frank confirm. I would like him to be my doctor." Standing she added, "I'll go see if he is free now. You go rest and we will catch up soon."

Allie sat at the table for a while after Emma left. She felt exhausted, but she also felt broken. She knew she should have been more hospitable towards her friend and her ma would have given her an ear full over that. She just couldn't find the energy to, though. Allie carried herself up the stairs and put herself in bed. It didn't take long for Frank to find her.

"Emma said I should find you. She wanted me to check on you." Frank came and sat at the edge of the bed.

"I'm ok," she lied. "Just tired again," so she only told a half lie.

Frank checked her over briefly, just to be sure she wasn't coming down with something and left her to sleep. Allie slept fitfully and remained in bed through dinner. Frank didn't press her. By the time he climbed into bed for the evening, she had found her deep slumber.

CHAPTER 27

Allie woke the next morning needing to hear from her ma. Emma's news left her feeling like she was back with Eddie and he'd punched her in the stomach...again.

She went about and did the morning chores as quickly as possible so she could spend the afternoon reading. She had already learned so much about her ma in the few times she read and she was anxious to read more.

So far, she discovered her ma had lived in a wealthy home where Allie's grandparents worked. She grew up with the children of her parents' employers. Her ma hadn't mentioned anything specific about her childhood before her sixteenth birthday when she received the journal, but Allie could form ideas of what life would have been like with the information she did give.

After that first entry, her ma had written sometimes weekly, sometimes more. It seemed once she turned sixteen, her daily lessons shifted from needlepoint, arithmetic, literacy, and how to act like a lady and compose oneself in polite society, to more specific duties of running a household and lessons in marital life.

Allie's grandmother was training her ma in the same fashion as Mrs. Richardson's children. Her grandmother was working towards bettering her ma's life. How she came to wed Pa, she didn't know yet, but hoped she was getting closer to that answer. Allie opened the journal and read the next entry dated December tenth, one thousand eight hundred eighty-two.

Oh, mother is pushing me. Christmas is right around the corner and I am working to make sure all of the gifts are made and ready, but mother keeps pulling me away to focus on lessons. I am not sure why she seems to be so determined that I learn all of this as quickly as possible, but Helen just marrying might have something to do with it.

I overheard mother and father speaking in private about my age and needing to cautiously guide me through this delicate portion of my life to ensure an appropriate outcome. I'm not sure what outcome they are hoping for.

Helen procured a suitor and now a husband when her parents held her first ball to introduce their daughter to the available gentlemen. Being of a lower class, I am aware I will not enjoy the same. How mother and father plan to wed me to someone above us is beyond me. I really don't care about the money or life, I simply want love. I have seen what love looks like amongst some of the other staff and others in the community. I've seen it enough to know that I much prefer that over the life of wealth. True happiness could not always be found within the higher class.

Now I'm rambling and wasting my time on my gift making. I am crocheting a lap blanket for Helen in the colors she chose for her wedding. I hope she will think of her wedding and smile every time she uses it.

For William, their oldest child and only son, I am knitting a scarf to go with a new suit he just purchased. He is four years older than I and preparing to start his own life.

Cassie, the youngest, and younger than myself by a year, will be getting stationary that I am making. I dried rose petals from last summer and am pressing them into the paper. Her gift is my favorite to work on. Each page is unique and beautiful. I must go and continue my work since mother has decided to leave me be for now, being that it is the Sabbath and lessons are withheld.

Allie smiled at the thought of her ma working on those gifts. She loved to make things with her hands, and now she knew how she developed her skills for her embroidery and quilting that she continued. It seemed Ma had many talents, some Allie hadn't known before. She continued reading with the next entry dated December fifteenth one thousand eight hundred eighty-two.

Did I meet my future husband today? Mother allowed me to venture into town with William as chaperone and purchase more yarn. I failed to purchase enough to finish my blanket project for Helen and was worrying that I wouldn't have time to finish it. At least I don't have to spin my own and can afford to buy it.

William saw me safe and sound to the entrance of the shop, but refused to go in. Instead he said he had his own shopping to do and would retrieve me soon. Since I knew exactly what I needed, my purchase didn't take any time at all.

I stepped out and decided to wait for him, not knowing exactly how long that might take. After standing only a few minutes a young man approached me. He had such a warmth to his smile and light in his eyes. I was lost for words for a moment and was nervous at first, not knowing him, but he was so kind.

He was concerned for me being alone. I told him about William and he decided he would wait with me until he returned. Oh, the way he cared for me and spoke to me with interest in what I had to say. No man had ever cared what I thought on most matters before. After I had carried on so, he asked me all kinds of questions and truly wanted my opinions. He was very sweet and handsome. Mother is going to be irate, but we made plans to meet again. I don't know much about him, but I plan to learn everything. We arranged a time to meet after Christmas and now I must find a way to make that work!

Nothing else was written for that day and Allie was extremely curious to know who this man was. She knew her ma and pa met while passing by on the street. One meeting lead to more which led to marriage. This sounded like it was Pa. She turned the page and found it dated after Christmas, December twenty eighth one thousand eight hundred eighty-two.

Christmas is always a busy time with preparations for the Richardson's annual feasting. The twenty-fifth is spent with just family, the twenty-sixth is a lavish party for their closest friends, and the twenty-seventh is a celebration for the staff. They allow the staff to take over the dining room and have a full Christmas meal. The staff still prepares it all first, though.

I am tired. I don't normally help in the kitchen, but when times get busy, I do what I can. Mother doesn't like me having to do any work that toughens my hands or makes me perspire, but I refuse to be served by my friends and equals, regardless of what mother wishes.

Now that all of that is over, I can finally relax. There will be no more lessons until after the New Year. I am free to do what I wish. Normally, I lay around and read, recouping from the laborious work.

The whole staff gets the time off, except for the essentials that must be done to keep the house running. Today was the day I was to meet my future. I spoke to Mother about taking a stroll through the city park. She refused at first, of course, stating that I needed a chaperone and she wasn't up for it just after the last three days.

I had already enlisted Helen, who agreed during Christmas. Helen was married now and could serve as chaperone. On the walk to the park, I explained to Helen my original motives for wanting to visit the park. She was angry at first, but upon telling her my last story, she decided she needed to meet the boy. I'd struck her curiosity.

When we arrived, I noticed he was already waiting for me. I made the introductions. Helen sat on the end of the bench and allowed me to sit in the middle. We conversed for an hour before he needed to take his leave. I learned about his family and how he grew up and he learned about mine. Helen seemed interested but remained mostly silent.

He asked if we could meet again and Helen answered for me. She is going to allow us to meet again at her home, under her supervision, of course. On the way home, she talked about how she felt when she first met her husband. She claimed that she could see that in me. Mother can't know. I am sure she wouldn't approve, even though everything will stay proper. I am not sure what will happen with this, but I can't wait to find out.

Allie closed the book feeling sweetly sad. Her parents had talked about how they met, but they left out so many details. Sweet details. Both Ma and Pa were hard working folks. They had been hardened on the outside from a tough life.

Allie would have never guessed this was their start. She was overjoyed getting to hear it now. If she could continue to read she would, but the supper hour was drawing near and she had work to do. She set the journal on the table for another time and went back to work, with the words of her ma replaying in her head and a smile upon her face.

CHAPTER 28

Over the next few days Allie continued taking naps in the afternoon. She had been through much in the last several weeks and Frank was thankful she was resting. Tears had been a regular occurrence. Frank had witnessed the grieving process from an outsider's perspective may times.

Being a doctor allowed him to see the beginnings and endings of life. He saw joy and grief on a regular basis. The more times he witnessed it, the more a wall went up. He was increasingly able to separate himself from such grief, mostly. His emotions were present, but not at the level in which the loved ones experienced. Watching his beloved go through it broke his heart. One minute she would be fine, smiling, and the next something would spark a memory or thought and she would either cry or become angry. He didn't take any of it personally, but he did hope that this portion would soon end.

Today was no different. By the middle of the day, Allie had already circled through her emotions twice. Frank was trying to be patient, but he found he needed a break. He was deeply saddened when Ma died, but the toll this took on Allie was crushing. Her spirit, the very essence that made her who she was had vanished. When he thought he could see her returning she would disappear again.

Frank was tired. Knowing that grief was something no one could avoid, he knew she must work through it all. He really didn't know how to help her, though. He hugged her when she cried, let her yell when she was angry, and tried to make her laugh as many times as he could. This afternoon he was called away from the office and wouldn't be around to see to her needs for a while.

Roger had stopped in and summoned Frank to his house. He hadn't said much other than Alex was sick and needed to be seen. Little kids getting sick was normal. Without knowing specifics, he wasn't sure if he would be tending to a tummy ache from eating too many sweets or a childhood disease. He hoped it was the first or something else minor.

Walking up to his bed, his stomach sank as he knew it was the latter. Alex was pale and clammy, which were all the signs of a fever. Emma had briefed Frank on Alex's bowel issues in addition to the fever and complaints of sore throat. Lifting his shirt revealed the rash he'd hoped he wouldn't see. Alex had all the signs of typhoid. He patted Alex on the hand and explained that he needed to speak to his parents and then would be right back. Frank, Roger and Emma all stepped out of the room and gently closed the door behind.

"There is no easy was to say this, so I'm just going to say it. Alex has typhoid," Frank said as he placed his hand on Roger's shoulder.

Emma sucked in air and Roger stared unmoving.

"What, what do we do?" Emma stuttered with the swells of tears beginning.

Frank thought for a moment.

"First, we quarantine. Emma, I know you want to be with him, but you are with child. You need to think about your other children as well."

Emma started to sob and Roger held her against him. They both stared at Frank.

"Then, we work on bringing down his fever and making him more comfortable. I have a few things I'm going to give him. One is to help with the fever. Another is to control the diarrhea. He is going to need to have boiled water ready to drink. Emma you can keep up on that while still staying away."

Emma nodded.

"Another way you can help is making sure there is a steady supply of strong meals. Once we bring this fever down he will need to eat to keep up his strength."

Emma rubbed her hands together nervously. "I can do all of that."

"Good. Roger can help me, but that means he will have no contact with you until this is all over." Frank looked between them.

Roger gave Emma a kiss on the forehead and then looked at Frank as though he was preparing for battle.

"All right, then. Roger we will need to get him in a lukewarm bath."

The men talked as they headed back into the room and Emma went the opposite way to begin on her tasks.

Hours passed and the men took turns wiping down Alex's body. His fever had lessoned, but was not gone. Typhoid could last weeks, and Frank knew they were just starting this battle.

"Roger, we need to get a schedule going. Sleep will be needed by both of us in order to get him through this."

Roger agreed, already feeling tired, but not wanting to sleep.

"You take the day shifts and I'll do nights. Teach me what to do."

Frank thought that was the best plan considering. Frank found paper and pencil and wrote down the instructions as he taught Roger.

"I'm going to go home and inform Allie. I'm sure she is beside herself not knowing where I am. I'm coming back here to sleep, though. I know we both need to rest, but I will sleep better here than clear at my house. Then if something isn't right, I'm here for you to wake."

Roger stuck out his hand to shake Frank's, but decided to pull him in for a hug instead. Frank was the one keeping his son alive at the moment. He already owed him everything. They parted and Frank rushed home as quickly as he could. When he walked through the door Allie rushed to greet him

"I've been worried sick. Supper was hours ago. It's pitch black outside."

Frank squeezed her tight.

"That's the life of a doctor's wife. I'm so sorry my dear. I was out on a call."

Allie stepped out of the embrace.

"That was what I was hoping. My mind was racing in all different directions about what could have happened."

Frank rubbed the back of his neck not sure how to tell her what he needed to.

"Are you hungry? I saved food." Allie started heading to the kitchen, but Frank stopped her.

"No, Emma fed me." He waited until the realization showed in her eyes.

"Emma? Why were you there?"

"Come, sit." They both took the chairs in the living room before Frank continued. "Alex is sick. I've been there all afternoon and into the evening." Frank blew out a breath. "Allie, it's typhoid."

Allie gasped and covered her mouth with her hand. A moment later she dropped her hand.

"How is he?"

Frank ran his hand down his face attempting and failing to wipe off the tired.

"He has a long way to go. I left him with Roger. Emma has been instructed not to go near him. I'm heading back over."

Allie held an expression of confusion and worry.

"Roger and I decided to take turns with him. I'll be sleeping over there until this is over."

Allie nodded, and tears started to fall.

"Oh, Emma!" Silently she wanted to hit her head against the wall. She had been jealous of Emma and now her son's life was in jeopardy. She was a horrible awful person. "Is there anything I can do?"

Frank thought on that for a moment.

"Yes, I think there might be. Emma is beside herself and pacing the floors since she isn't allowed in. Maybe I can convince her to spend time with you daily. That will break up her days and hopefully keep her sane. Being with child, she needs to keep up her health."

Frank knew they both needed a distraction from their worries. If he couldn't help Allie, perhaps this would be some reprieve in its own way.

"Of course," Allie bobbed her head. "You will need things, change of clothing, blankets..." Allie raced up the stairs and began packing for him.

Frank followed dragging his heels. He was tired, but liked seeing that Allie had some energy. She had been so tired lately. Maybe she had moved past that. Frank was leaving Allie again when she needed him, but this time he knew he needed to.

Something told him she would be fine, he could feel that. With Alex was where Frank was supposed to be for the time being. Frank took the bag from Allie and, after kissing her goodbye, headed as quickly as possible back to Alex.

CHAPTER 29

Allie paced the floor for days. Emma had come daily and Allie tried to find things to talk about that would distract her, but nothing worked. Emma was scared, and Allie was too. Keeping busy was the only way to keep her calm. They worked in the kitchen, tended the garden, and walked through town. During one of their walks, Emma asked Allie a question that pained her.

"Having Alex like this made me so scared. We need to plan for the possibility of more of us getting sick. What if Roger and I get sick and don't make it? What would happen to our children if they are fine?"

"Emma, let's not talk like that right now. Let's focus on just today." Allie's eyebrows furrowed with concern.

Emma stopped walking and turned Allie towards her.

"No! You are not a mother, so you don't understand the importance of having a plan. I don't want anyone else to decide the future of my children."

Allie cringed and she grew cold as she felt the blow Emma's words caused.

Emma grasped Allie's shoulders and looked into her eyes and continued.

"This place, this life is all my children know. We have no family close by. I don't want them shipped across states when they are dealing with the worst thing that could ever happen to them. They barely know either of our families. They know here. I want them to stay here."

"But how? They can't live on their own." Allie was confused, perhaps still off guard from the reminder she was not a mother.

Emma moved her soft hand to Allie's cheek.

"With you Allie. You and Frank. God forbid should anything happen to both of us. Oh please, say you would take them and raise them as your own."

Allie sucked in air, her eyes moving between Emma's trying to find the truth that lay within. "You are being silly. The likelihood that both of you would be gone is low." Allie pulled away and took a few steps, eyes on her shoes.

"Allie, I'm not being silly. Yes, let's hope that it never comes to that, but I need to know they have somewhere to go. Somewhere they already know so they won't be as scared."

"Oh Emma," Allie turned back to her and embraced her. "Of course, we would do that."

Her heart did a tiny flutter at the dream of having

children, but she quickly beat it down as the cost of losing a friend was no price, no option. She wanted children, but she would never hope for the death of their parents to have that. Emma and Allie pulled back from each other, both wiping their own tears.

Later in the day Allie had returned to her ma's journal. Emma's words remained in the back of her mind as she read on. She was touched that Emma would think of her and trust her, but hoped that would never be needed. Allie kept reading while her mind was divided between the two. She almost missed the significance of the passage and started again fully focused in order to follow.

May thirteenth one thousand eight hundred eighty-three,

Mother has discovered my secret. Allen and I had been meeting regularly at Helen's home and no one was the wiser until today when Mrs. Richardson decided to make a drop in visit to her daughter's home. She walked in on us sitting in the morning room drinking tea.

After both Helen and I heard an ear full, she immediately went straight to my mother informing her. Allen followed Helen and I home. Mother was livid. I, of course, already knew she would be, which was why I wished to keep this secret.

During her ranting and raving she let slip that her hopes were for me to marry William, the Richardson's son. Everyone was shocked upon hearing that, and mother was left stammering.

Mrs. Richardson's jaw dropped before quickly putting mother in her place. Her son would not marry below him, leaving my mother visibly much smaller than usual.

Allen had remained against the wall, trying to blend in to the surroundings as much as possible, until this moment when he appeared beside me and linked his hand with mine. That moment was when my whole world changed. Allen spoke up and proclaimed his love for me. He asked me to marry him, which I accepted, and that sent my mother into another round of fits.

Mrs. Richardson intervened and spoke up for me. She put mother in her place like only she could. Mother turned from livid to outright rage. I have never seen her so angry. She spit through clinched teeth that if Allen was what I wanted, to do it, but to do it quickly.

I didn't hesitate. I ran to my room, gathered what I could fit into a trunk and Allen carried it out of the house into his wagon. Mother left to her room and refused to see me leave. I climbed into the wagon, instead of a coach that mother would have preferred, and into my new life. I can't help but feel torn between my mother and Allen, but this man seems to offer more love in this moment.

Allie was stunned. She now knew why she never knew much of her grandparents on Ma's side. She also knew why Ma rarely mentioned anything about them and kept it fairly vague when she did. Allie was saddened by learning these details. Closing the door on everything and everyone you knew must have been terrifying. Allie wasn't sure she could have done the same.

Then a thought struck her. She had done something somewhat similar. Her parents didn't turn against her, but she made a rash decision and married someone she barely knew. Ma was concerned about it, but she didn't stand in Allie's way. It now made perfect sense why Ma let her go.

Allie was glad that she had a home to go back to when the realization of the mistake she made became branded all over her body. She knew the outcome of Ma's choice. She and Pa were happy and had a wonderful life.

Then again, Allie began wondering how wonderful it really was. Ma kept all of this from her and that made her wonder if there was more left hidden. She didn't have the energy to keep reading tonight. Allie was drained once again and decided since it was just her, she would skip dinner and just go straight to bed. She hoped someday soon her energy would return and her emotions would settle. She knew why she was a wreck, but couldn't control it despite knowing the cause. She had been taken over by grief and was being manipulated by it and was just too tired to fight it.

CHAPTER 30

Frank had no clue what day it was. He had lost track many days ago. It was looking like Alex was pulling through, and the whole house's nervous excitement was palpable. No one else had developed any symptoms for which Frank silently gave thanks. Alex's fever was down, and he was hungry. Emma kept a steady stream of hot food at the ready for him to enjoy.

"Emma, I think it's safe to say you may go see your son," Frank happily announced. He was thrilled he could say those words to her instead of the alternate of how this could have played out.

"Thank you, thank you, thank you," Emma beamed. "I really don't know how to show you how thankful I am, Frank!"

Emma gleefully wrapped her arms around him and Roger cleared his throat. Emma released Frank and he could see her rosy complexion return to a once worrisome face. She then went and stood by Roger and held his hand.

"I agree with Emma. What can we do for you?" Roger

shook Frank's hand with a firm grip.

Frank sighed, he was tired.

"Nothing. This is my job and Alex's recovery is enough for me."

"You are a good man, Frank, but I will think of something. You have to make a living doing this, too." One of their roosters out back crowed. "Ah, that gives me an idea. I think a small flock might be in order."

Frank laughed. "Well, fresh eggs are sure nice, but I'm not sure where we would keep them." He said his goodbyes and reassured that he would come back every day for the next few days to make sure Alex kept improving. Then it was time to head home to Allie.

He dragged his heels all the way back to Wiley City. He was tired enough he could have curled up on the way and slept for a while, but knew he needed to get home. He reached his house after what seemed like hours of walking, plopped into a chair in the living room, and immediately fell into slumber.

Allie was headed home from grabbing the mail. A letter from Blinne came and she was excited to read it. Not willing to wait until she was home, she ripped the envelope open and began reading as she strolled home.

Dearest Allie,

I hope this letter finds you well and rested. I didn't say anything when you were here, but I did worry about you. Often times the caregiver in the end needs more care than the patient. You worked yourself too hard, but I can't say that I blame you. I would have done the same. I miss you even though I am glad to know that you are home and able to focus on yourself.

I miss your Ma. I have been to the farm a few times to check on your Pa and Drew, always bringing some food with me as my reason for stopping in. I know Pa enjoys what I bring. He is sad, but the farm seems to be running fine. The house itself isn't running as smoothly as it would have been, but they seem to be managing. It's nothing too bad, but there were some unwashed dishes on the counter and the floor hadn't been swept recently. I am sure that in time they will settle into a good solid routine and the upkeep will improve.

Your brother is the same ole Drew. He talks to me more now than he did before. He is proud of what he is doing to help Pa and has grabbed my hand a time or two to lead me around and show me his work. I am not concerned about him at all. He is going to be just fine. I'm not really concerned about Pa, either, but I know that he is hurting and it's going to take time to find joy again. I will continue to drop in and make sure things keep improving.

I have grown larger since the last time you saw me. I'm ready for this to be done. My feet are swelling, and I have to rest frequently. I don't remember being this large with Lena. Doc is telling me that everything is looking good. He is encouraging me to sit often and put my feet up. He says the swelling is from water retention and if I elevate I can help it drain. George has made a routine of nightly foot rubs. They are heavenly. Lena is continuing to grow like a weed. She is crawling everywhere and getting into everything. Simple things amuse her and her laugh is adorable.

I am sending my love with this letter. Please take care of yourself and I look forward to hearing back from you.

Love you,

Blinne

Allie stuffed the letter back in the envelope and wiped a tear off her cheek. She hadn't realized until after she'd finished reading that she was crying or that she was nearly home. Pa's sadness increased her own, and Allie was tired of being sad. Knowing that Drew was doing fine helped, though.

Allie made her way up the front steps and walked through the door. She spotted Frank slumped back, arms folded loosely on his chest, sleeping in the chair. Frank being home made her wonder what that meant for Alex. She hoped it was good. She grabbed a lap quilt and draped it over him. He woke with the touch, somewhat startled but still in a daze.

"Hi," Allie greeted, placing her lips on his forehead.

Frank stretched and grabbed the back of his neck with a moan.

"Hi. Sleeping here sure gave me a kink in my neck. I'm surprised I made it this far and didn't doze in the entry," Frank joked.

"Why don't you go upstairs then and get some quality sleep?"

Frank nodded. "I just might." His stomach rumbled and he patted it. "It seems I'm a tad hungry."

"Well, that I can take care of. Follow me."

She pulled him up out of the chair and headed to the kitchen, motioning for Frank to sit. She cut off a slice of bread she had made the day before and slathered some butter on it before handing it to him. Frank ate about half of it before she asked about Alex.

"Since you are home, that must mean that Alex didn't need your complete attention anymore?" She was hopeful while trying to prepare for bad news.

Frank nodded and swallowed.

"Yes, he is doing much better and no one else has shown any symptoms. I did tell them that I would stop in daily to continue checking progress."

"That is wonderful news! I bet Emma is beside herself with joy. I tried to help her when she was here, but I can't imagine what she was going through. Well, I suppose I can somewhat relate." Allie said as she folded a dish cloth.

"How were things around here?" Frank got up and fetched himself a glass of water.

Allie returned focus to the conversation and took a seat opposite Frank's chair as he made his way back to the table.

"Mostly boring, except when Emma was here, and when I was telling patients that you were away for a while."

"Were there many?"

"A few, but nothing seemed serious. I would have told them where to find you if I thought any of them needed immediate attention."

"Spoken like a true doctor's wife. Already triaging."

Allie blushed. "Oh, Frank, it wasn't that big of a deal. I do need to talk to you about something Emma asked me, and I did get a letter from Blinne. That's what I was doing just now."

Frank leaned back in his chair waiting for the news. "And?"

"Which one, Emma or the letter?"

"The letter. I'm curious to know how your family is doing back home."

"It's all alright. She says that Pa is sad, but Drew seems just fine."

Frank looked at her a minute trying to gauge how Allie was doing. He hadn't seen her in days and hoped that she had improved. He couldn't decide and thought his exhaustion might be the cause.

"That's to be expected for Pa, and I am happy to hear Drew is doing well."

"The letter didn't really give me any information that I wasn't expecting so that is good."

Frank nodded.

"That's great news. I'm glad that they are moving on and living. So, what did Emma want? I know she was beside herself the entire time she couldn't be with Alex."

Emma took a deep breath and began.

"Yes, she really wasn't herself. I'm relieved to know that things are better. She needed them to be. I was concerned the whole time for her unborn with all her fretting and worrying. I don't think she got much sleep."

"No, she didn't," Frank confirmed. "What did she want, though? If I didn't know any better, I'd think you were stalling."

Emma smirked. "Well, I think Alex being so sick scared her."

"Of course it scared her, but you still haven't told me what she discussed with you," Frank pursued, raising his eyebrows and pursing his lips.

Allie fidgeted with her hands.

"She asked if we would take their children and raise them as ours if anything should happen to her and Roger. And, I sort of said yes without thinking to ask you first." She looked at Frank with a concerned look not sure how he would take that.

Frank folded his hands. "I see. Why wouldn't she want them with family?"

Allie stood and paced.

"I asked that as well. She said there was no family close enough and she didn't want the kids removed from the only environment they know while dealing with that kind of loss."

Frank walked to her and gently grabbed her shoulder to halt her pacing.

"Allie, you will wear a whole in the floor if you keep this up."

Allie stopped walking but looked down at the floor, too nervous to see his expression.

Frank lifted her chin to look into her eyes.

"Of course, we will take them. You were right to tell her yes."

Allie released a breath she didn't realize she'd been holding and a smile crossed her face.

"Oh Frank, I'm so glad you said that. Of course I told her she was talking nonsense and nothing would come of it, but I was worried you wouldn't want the potential of others' children being our responsibility."

Frank chuckled a bit.

"Allie, I'm a doctor. Others' kids from time to time are my responsibility. The only difference with this would be I wouldn't transfer that duty back when they were healthy. I truly am happy you said yes. We haven't known them long, but those kids are growing on me." Frank rubbed his eyes. "No, of course, it will never come to that, but my answer will always be yes should the unimaginable happen."

Allie squeezed him. "Thank you for agreeing and not being upset with me."

"I could never be upset with you, my dear," he yawned mid-sentence.

"You look tired. Why don't you go to bed?"

"So do you. Why don't you come to bed with me?"

"Alright. Let me clean up in here first, and I'll meet you up there."

Frank nodded and headed upstairs. By the time Allie made it up, Frank was sound asleep. Allie smiled sweetly. She pulled the covers back on her side and slipped carefully into bed so as not to wake him. She felt at peace knowing that her family was doing as expected and Frank was home. She drifted into a much needed slumber.

CHAPTER 31

During the next few days life for Frank and Allie returned to normal, or at least what the new normal was after Ma died. Frank thought Allie seemed to be getting worse instead of better, but he wasn't ready to say anything to her. She was still taking naps throughout the day and her mood swings were all over the place.

Frank would wake in the morning to one Allie and by lunch she would be a different version. Little things could bring on tears or anger. Sometimes, something he said would trigger it, or if something in the day didn't go as planned, she would break down, unable to handle it. Frank hoped this was all just due to him being gone and Allie dealing with the worry for Alex on top of the passing of her Ma.

Knowing all of this made today difficult. Frank left Allie alone while he went to North Yakima to pass along the latest typhoid case and he hoped he would hear progress on discovering the cause of this epidemic.

He would love to meet with Mr. Lumsden, but Dr. Green would suffice, if he was the only one available. Mr. Lumsden was on a mission and had a big task. Frank knew his time was precious as it should be. The sooner the cause could be discovered, the more lives could be saved.

He took the trolley from Wiley City and would walk through town. He wanted to get a better view and feel of the city. There were clues to be found, he just needed to be observant to catch them.

He stepped off the trolley and straight into the rush of the daily crowd. As he made his way through town he saw many opportunities of where typhoid could have spread. The local dairies brought their cows through and around town. Their droppings left behind for whomever to step in were a perfect breeding ground for disease. Flies were also thick in many places.

Frank was curious about the city's water supply. If it was anywhere near any of the dairies that could explain the typhoid spread. Of course, an establishment with unsanitary conditions could be the culprit, but that wouldn't explain Alex getting it. All those cases would be connected and traceable. Unless perhaps contracted through contact with the sick. He rounded the corner and walked through Dr. Green's office door. He quickly surmised that no one was around by the stillness in the room. Frank sighed, not sure what to do next. He stepped back out on the street and almost ran straight into Dr. Green himself.

"Hello, Dr. Green," Frank held out his hand.

"Hi Frank. It's Henry. Here we're equals," The men shook hands, "Follow me, let's get out of the street so we can talk."

They made their way back into Henry's office. He offered Frank a glass of water. Summer was always warm in this country and Henry kept water at the ready. Frank thanked him and took a good long drink.

"What brings you by today, Frank?"

"Well, I was hoping to get some information on the latest of the epidemic. Also, I wanted to inform you of a typhoid patient I treated."

Henry pulled his glasses off, fogged them with a breath, and cleaned them on his shirt. He motioned for Frank to take a seat and sat with him.

"I'm beginning to lose my patience with this epidemic. I just came from checking on a few patients with typhoid myself. Tell me about your patient."

"Luckily, my patient lives."

Henry nodded at Frank's words and looked visibly relieved.

"Alex is a little two-year-old boy. I stayed at his house, along with his father. We worked around the clock, taking turns to treat him."

Henry's eyes shot up.

"That is dedication and probably what saved him. Between the fever and the bowel issues it's a wonder any of them can be saved."

"I wouldn't have done anything different. This particular boy's parents are friends of mine and my missus."

"Well, in that case, I'm even happier to hear of the positive outcome," Henry stated and moved to his files. He pulled out a folder and handed it to Frank. "These here are the cases I have treated as of late."

Frank felt the weight of the folder before opening it to the many pages it held. "This is impressive, but not in a good way."

Henry rubbed his neck. "Trust me, I know. Several of those people are no longer with us."

Frank scanned the pages and continued asking questions.

"Has Mr. Lumsden been able to connect any dots? Have you, through these?

"Nothing significant, yet. We are both working towards an answer. I want you to write your case down to add to this. I need everything, so we can compare them all."

"Of course. Anything I can do, I will." Frank closed the folder. "What has Mr. Lumsden said so far?"

"That the city is dirty," Henry chuckled sarcastically. "That is the only fact he's been able to come up with. Of course it's dirty. Anyone with eyes can see that," he paused and sighed. "He has started taking action on the cleanup, though."

"Well, that's something. I've been telling everyone who will listen to boil water. What are people supposed to do here?"

Henry sat back down next to Frank.

"Boiling water is good. I've also been encouraging folks to do that. He has suggested we move the privies further away from the wells. He has noted the dairies unsanitary habits and instructed correction."

"One dairy was placing full bottles of milk in the river to cool them. The problem with that is the river is visibly contaminated with animal excrement and other garbage. I wouldn't think of eating a trout out of it. Another dairy had dead flies in numbers as he had never seen before. Those were to be removed in addition to traps being placed all over town."

"The local women's groups are banding together to help clean things up and a sanitation league is forming. There is also talk of the city developing some type of sewage system. No city around for miles and miles that I can tell has one, so if North Yakima can produce that we will be ahead of our time here."

Frank was stunned at the proposals for clean-up.

"Wow! That's a lot of work being done. Sure, we don't have the actual cause figured out, but with all of that taking place the numbers are bound to decrease."

Henry sure hoped so. Things needed to change direction before a full pandemic exploded.

"I can take that information back to Wiley City and make sure we're doing all we can there as well to prevent any more cases," Frank added.

"That's a good plan, Frank. I'm helping here with cleaning things up when I can, but my practice has me running most of the time. How is yours going?"

Frank's lips turned up a bit thinking about his practice.

"Things are going smoothly. I'm not overly busy, but I do have enough to sustain me for now. I would like to grow and be able to purchase a home or some land and build, but for now we are comfortable. Our landlord is a very generous man, so that also helps."

"That sounds good. I'm very glad you chose to settle here in the area. This place seems to grow daily, and we can use all the help we can get." Henry heard a cow moo outside and he started laughing. "You run in with animals as payment yet?"

Frank belly laughed. "No, not yet, but I do have one patient that mentioned building a chicken coup and supplying the first hens for me. I could use them. For now we are buying our eggs."

"My farm was set up by my patients a long time ago. Now, I give away the animals to those in need," Henry sounded relieved. After all, how could a doctor have time to be a successful farmer anyway?

Frank nodded knowing the desire for a patient to clear his bill anyway he could. He was just happy that he could occasionally accept that form of payment and still survive, providing the necessities for he and Allie.

The door opened and both men turned to see who entered.

"Hello, may I help you?" Henry addressed a grey-haired woman as Frank made his way out the door with a silent wave good-bye.

Frank headed back to Wiley City the same way he arrived. He was encouraged to know progress was being made. They didn't have solid answers yet, but he knew things were going in the right direction, at least.

When he arrived home, Allie was in the kitchen with a bright cheery smile on her face. Frank wrapped his arms around her waist.

"Hello my sweet."

"Why, hello dear," Allie squeezed him back before they separated.

Frank proceeded telling her the new information he'd learned on his little trip, which only brightened her mood further.

"Did anything happen while I was gone?"

Allie thought the day over.

"Not really. There were a few people here to see you, but they will be back tomorrow. You did have one visitor that struck me as odd though."

Frank's brows drew together.

"Oh really? Who might that have been?"

"A sister, from the convent. She said she was seeking help or advice on how to treat the natives."

Frank thought for a moment. "Did she give you any

other information?"

"No nothing. She just said she would return again when she could and hoped you would be here then."

There were any number of things she might need assistance with that came to mind. There was one he hoped wasn't the reason. Typhoid. He would find out soon enough. His gut told him he needed to make sure he was well rested before she came knocking again. If it was what he was hoping it wasn't, he could be gone much longer than he was when he tended to Alex.

"Thanks Allie. I'm going to head to the office. Dr. Green requested that I write my report down on Alex for him. I'll get that done and post it to him. I need to stay around here to make sure I'm available when the sister returns."

Allie kissed his cheek and returned to work, humming while she did. Frank's worry eased a bit by her mood and the sweet sounds she was making. He left feeling hopeful that his earlier worry was all for naught and that she was actually improving.

CHAPTER 32

The days had long past warm and were now stifling.
Allie awakened early to finish the bulk of her daily chores before
the heat really kicked in. There was only one place she knew to
go to get some relief from the heat. Allie gathered her Bible and
her ma's journal before making her way to the creek.

She removed her shoes and stockings and dipped her
feet in the water. The cool rushing water gave instant relief and
she sighed while she closed her eyes and enjoyed the refreshing
chill that crept up her legs. If she were back home, she would
strip her clothes down and let the water cover her whole body.
She wasn't though. The road was just to her right and anyone
traveling by could see her. What was exposed was already too
much, but she didn't care. There had to be exceptions made
when the conditions were extreme.

She reached over and picked up her Bible and opened
to Ecclesiastes. She read a while, finding portions that stood out
to her here and there. "One generation passeth away and
another generation cometh"... "Whirleth about continually"...it
was all a circular effect.

Allie was one to break that circle. Her ma passed, and her child did too. Allie was the end. She continued reading, but thoughts kept circling in her head, wondering if she was living for herself again or if she truly and fully was following God's plan.

Was her desire to have a child from the Lord, or was she just seeking to fill a void or fill the next natural step after marriage? Allie always thought she wanted children, but when she married Eddie a need grew inside her. Then the devastating loss came with the news of potentially no others.

She didn't understand why God would allow this yearning to live in her heart if nothing was ever to come of it. She read without paying attention until she stopped on chapter three verse eleven. "He hath made every thing beautiful in his time." It would all work out the way it was supposed to work out. Allie needed to remember that. Staying focused on living each day for Him and waiting for His guidance was the only way to move past this. Her ma would have helped, though. She desperately missed her.

Allie exchanged her Bible for Ma's journal, needing to hear her voice. She had read here and there over the last couple of weeks and discovered more about her parents in the process. Not knowing where to go after they left in a rush, Pa took her home to his folks'. He introduced her as his fiancé, which set Ma back a bit.

She hadn't thought about what would happen after she left the only home she had ever known and wasn't sure she was ready to move ahead that quickly. But the path had already been set. Pa's parents took it the way most would. They were surprised, shocked, and then insistent that the wedding took place quickly. They were good people, but having an unwed non-relative living with them would set tongues to wagging. So, they did. Given that Ma was over sixteen, she didn't need her parents to sign for the marriage. They were wed by Pa's family's preacher a week after she moved in. Pa had slept in the barn until that night when he moved back into his room that Ma had occupied alone until the wedding.

Allie couldn't fathom what newly married and living under a stranger's roof would have been like. Moving from single to married was intimidating enough without having in-laws overseeing every second of it.

Allie wasn't surprised when she read a bit farther and learned they decided to make a new life for themselves in Montana. Pa knew the railroad would be hiring and they wanted some space and privacy. Allie didn't know that Pa had worked on the railroad. Why he never said anything to her regarding that was still a mystery.

November eighteenth, eighteen hundred eighty-three

It is cold in Montana and winter hasn't officially arrived yet. Allen was able to find work with the railroad and we have been given housing. I am very thankful for a place of our own. He works long hours and often is away for days at a time. I have a dry roof over my head, and he keeps the wood stocked for the fire, so I should be counting my blessings. I'm lonely, though. Women are scarce. I have an exciting secret that I will tell Allen when he returns next. I'm not sure how many months it will take, but I won't be lonely soon. A babe is on the way and I am terrified, but over the moon at the same time!

Allie paused. This couldn't be her as the year was wrong and Drew was younger. If Ma was not mistaken, she must have lost the baby. Miscarriages were common enough, but it never dawned on Allie before how much time there was between when her parents married and when she was born. Another untold part of her folks' story? Allie figured they must have been too mournful or perhaps sparing her the unpleasant parts of their past. She was beyond curious at this point and read on.

November twenty ninth, eighteen hundred eighty-three

The baby is gone. Allen was so excited to learn of my pregnancy, but he had to go back to work for an extended time and he doesn't know of the crushing news. It is our first and even though I know this is common, it still hurts. I was very excited to be a mother. We will move forward, though. I have spoken to the Lord much in the recent days and am reassured there will be other babies.

Allie's heart broke for her parents. They had never mentioned this to either Allie or Drew. She hoped Ma talked about it with someone. Allie knew from experience that it helped to talk about it. Though speaking to the Lord does bring some surety, a shoulder to cry on is a great comfort. Her ma was blunt and cold when she found out about Allie's loss. Knowing this information didn't make that sit well. Her ma would have known Allie's heartbreak. She should have sympathized with her. She didn't though. She turned hard and distant. Everything seemed murkier than before. Allie had hoped she would find answers, but instead she was more confused than ever. Answers would have to wait as footsteps approached and broke her concentration.

"Well, there you are," Frank sat down next to her.

"Hi. You scared me. I was lost in thought."

"I could tell. I closed the office and went looking for you. When I realized you weren't in the house or out in the garden, I knew right where to find you." He looked at the creek and smiled.

"I'm so hard to read, aren't I?" They both chuckled.

Frank wrapped one arm around her, snuggling her close.

"What have you been doing?"

Allie gathered her books in her lap. "Reading, thinking, remembering," she answered sadly.

Frank widened his eyes and remained silent, hoping she would continue. She didn't. They stayed that way for a while. He wished he knew how to help her, but if she didn't fully open up to him, he didn't have a chance.

"What do you say we head for home?" He asked, his stomach rumbled.

"Oh Frank. I bet it's later than I thought!" Allie's eyes widened, "You must be hungry, and I haven't started on dinner yet."

"It's alright. Sometimes it's good to get away and find time for sorting out life."

How she got so lucky with Frank she would never know. She hugged her books and leaned into Frank. Then his stomach rumbled again.

"Come on. It's time to go home. You can help me get something on the table so it doesn't take as long."

He helped her up, she fixed her attire, and they walked back home together in silence. She would tell Frank everything she had read and what she would read sometime soon, but she liked holding on to the information for herself for a bit first. She felt closer to her Ma that way. She could hold her secrets inside before releasing them. She had very little of her ma now, but this journal was a treasure. She was learning so much even though she was more confused than ever. Allie knew, somehow, that the answers she needed would be revealed. She just hoped they wouldn't be too painful to read.

CHAPTER 33

Frank was in the office when a knock sounded on the door. Frank opened it to see a woman dressed in full habit standing before him.

"Sister, good afternoon. What can I do for you?" He was expecting her to drop in at any point after Allie had told him a few days back that she had come looking for him when he wasn't home.

"Good afternoon, Dr. Hubbard. I'm glad to find you here. Last time I dropped in I spoke with your wife," she remained standing on the stoop.

"Ah, yes, Allie mentioned that to me," he stepped aside and gestured for her to enter. "Please, do come in."

"Thank you, Doctor," she stepped over the threshold and into the center of the room.

"What brings you by today?" Frank had been very curious since Allie had told him she stopped in.

"I've been serving at the reservation and we have a few illnesses that are getting worse despite my efforts. I was wondering if you had some time to come assess the situation and teach me what to do."

"I see," Frank said as he made his way to his chair. "Of course, I'll go and see what I can do. I need to let Allie know where I'll be. We are heading to the mission correct?"

"Not specifically, no. The mission hasn't been used for some time. We will be going to the reservation, though."

"Oh, I see. I knew there was a mission and I just assumed."

She folded her hands in front of her. "I'm sure you had no need before to know the history. If you'll go talk to your wife, I can catch you up on the way out." She appeared a tad antsy, knowing that some were gravely ill. Frank knew the urgency of his departure.

"Ah yes, of course. I'll be right back."

Frank found Allie and let her know the plan. He didn't know how long he would be gone and wished he didn't need to leave her again.

"It is the nature of your service Frank. They need you and that is not lost on me." Allie kissed him on the forehead and bid the doctor farewell.

Frank rejoined the sister after and inquired about her mode of transportation. Realizing she walked, he suggested they take his wagon and she didn't object. She moved quickly, and Frank was forced to rush himself to keep up. They hitched Penny in no time at all and were on their way south.

214

"You haven't been here long have you, Dr. Hubbard?"

"No ma'am, I've been here about eight months now. How'd you know?"

She smirked a bit. "Well for starters you thought the mission was still up and running. It's been closed for several years now."

"Sorry about that. I have been meaning to see if there was any need for a doctor within the native community. It seems that other events have gotten in the way of that."

"That's all right, Doctor. Not many intermingle. The Yakima are mostly a friendly nation, but it hasn't always been so."

Frank knew the struggles with whites and Indians mixing, but hadn't heard any specifics regarding these peoples.

"I haven't heard of any current troubles, things have settled down around here, right?"

"Mostly, yes. Pride runs deep, and wounds are slow to heal, but progress has been made."

"Please, tell me what you know. Maybe if I have a better understanding, it will help me, help them."

The sister adjusted in her seat and settled in for a while.

"There were several native groups that inhabited these lands: the Yakima, Palus, Wenatchi, Klikitat, Skinpah, and several more. They usually remained friendly - sharing, bartering, and even inter-marring. They were a people living here for many years before anyone else encroached on their lands.

"Then missionaries and trappers came. White men

brought their faith and ways with them. For a while it didn't matter. There was so much land to share and too few whites to Indians ratio to make a big impact. Then the government got involved and decided they wanted this land."

Frank could tell this woman truly sympathized with the natives.

The sister drew another breath and continued. "Back in the middle of the eighteen-hundreds the Indians formed two groups as a way of uniting to better fight for their land and ways to remain. There was a treaty, and leaders from all over came and eventually signed. Some were willing, and others pressured. The government traded their land for money and promises. They promised more money yearly, designated land set aside for just them, buildings such as sawmills, blacksmiths, schools, and so forth as well as the training to operate them."

"That sounds like a decent trade," Frank chimed in.

"Yes, it looked fairly good on paper. They were set to acquire much, but they also had to give much. No one really knew how much they would give until it was too late. Now, don't get me wrong, I love that we have been able to reform many of them. The problem is the government didn't hold up their whole end of the bargain. The Indians who were used to living off the land and traveling around to obtain what they need are now forced to remain in a smaller confinement that doesn't always provide. They are hungry and sick. We are doing what we can, but we are only a few. Then the fact that many white settlers have not always abided by the laws and trampled over their land even killing some as they go, has only added to the hurt and anger they feel." She looked around a bit and pointed. "You will want to turn left up here."

Frank followed. "How much farther?"

"Not far. We will start seeing homes soon. I have a couple of people I would like you to see today, but I am sure just about anywhere we stop you could find someone to treat."

Frank felt sad. He had put off meeting the needs of these people far too long. He came here to help whenever and however he was needed, and right now, he was only treating part of the population. He knew that had to change, today. He would need to earn these people's trust and after hearing what others like him had done, he was concerned that might be harder than he first thought.

"Have you been able to convert many?" Figuring out their beliefs and honoring those would be a good start on building trust.

"Some, yes. There are several, though, that refuse to give up some of their beliefs... such as keeping multiple wives. Changing one's ways is a difficult thing to do for anyone. Taking a whole culture and trying to turn it towards the Lord is a task that will take many more years, if ever, to accomplish. Meeting the needs, where they are now, is all we can hope for. Educating the young is helping with the future generations, though. It does make for some conflict in some families, but we have had the most success with the youth."

Frank knew the difficulty in changing. "Everyone has their own path and way to God. Some never make it and others do. The most successful ones seem to be the ones who move on God's time and not man's, though."

Sister looked up curiously at him, "And how did you

come to learn this?"

"Being a doctor gives me a personal inside view of many. People tend to share honestly when they feel safe and feel you can help them. A listening ear and some words of advice sometimes are all that's needed to heal the afflicted. You would be surprised how many physical ailments stem from heartache or stresses. Financial troubles, major life events and changes, big decisions that need made can cause headaches, heart palpitations, and stomach issues. Sometimes being a doctor means being a friend."

"I think you are going to be a good fit for these people. I hope they allow you in and give you a chance. Speaking of, the first house I would like to visit is just up the road on the right. Let me introduce you. Only some speak English and I will act as your interpreter."

The home she was referencing didn't look like what he anticipated. He shouldn't have formed any ideas of what he would see, though, as he knew these people lived a different way from him. Frank agreed and together they began working towards earning trust.

CHAPTER 34

Allie had no idea when Frank would be back. He didn't take anything with him that would indicate a lengthy stay, so she decided to plan for his return later in the evening. She knew as a doctor though, his plans and ideas could change at a moment's notice.

She moved through her day quickly. The days were long and hot which meant the garden work was done early morning and late evening, leaving the inside work to be completed during the hottest point in the day. The house upkeep didn't take much time at all. She kept up on the dust, but work in the garden and the kitchen took most of her time.

With the heat scorching down on them, watering the garden quickly became the biggest task, much as it had been on her parent's farm. It especially took more effort since Frank requested that the water they used for the edibles be boiled first. Allie had begun boiling pots of water the night before, so she could get a head start on how much was needed each day.

The hottest portion of the days coincided with the time

she felt she needed to rest a bit. She had begun taking her ma's journal to bed with her and reading at least one passage before taking a nap.

Frank was always busy with his practice in the middle of the afternoon, and as long as she woke early enough to prepare supper, he was clueless to how much she was sleeping. She was told that grief overtook your life, but until she lived it, she didn't fully understand. It drained her energy and she was still dealing with mood swings. She continued to pray that the worst would be over soon, and she would feel normal again. She knew her ma wouldn't want her overly fussing and carrying on for her. She was at peace and pain free and Allie should be feeling grateful for that. She missed her ma though. Allie ran a finger over the wings of the butterfly on the cover, then opened the journal and began the next entry.

June ninth, eighteen hundred eighty-four,

The weather continues to warm, and life is in full bloom. The land is gorgeous, and I am finding the area very welcoming. There are still more men in this area, but I am making friends with the few women. We are coming together regularly for coffee and started bringing our sewing and darning projects along to work on while we converse.

One of the women brings her embroidery work. She is expecting and said her family has a tradition of making the patch-work for each baby blanket. It makes that blanket special and unique, just like the baby.

I love this idea and have decided to include a version of this history for my own children. Instead of a patch that would then need to be fixed onto another piece of cloth for the blanket,

I am thinking of doing a quilt square. What to embroider is still a work in progress, but I am finding that I love the idea the more I think on it. And, since I should be a mother by Christmas time, I need to get a move on. I haven't said anything to anyone yet, given the loss we had last year, but figuring I'm somewhere around three months, I think it should be fairly safe now. Maybe I'll do a Christmas square since the babe should arrive around then. Whatever I decide, I'm sure the blanket will be lovely.

Allie was confused again. She crawled out from under the covers of her bed where she was reading and pulled out the quilt squares from her ma that she had stored under her bed. She sifted through them, but there was no Christmas one in the bunch. They were all just seasons. She grabbed the journal and skimmed the next couple of entries, but all that was there was the daily goings on and the mention of her ma's continued pregnancy. She flipped the page and read further to find a one-line entry dated July second, eighteen hundred eighty-four.

We have lost a second child and I am beside myself in grief.

Allie's heart broke again for her parents. Losing one was hard enough, but now the second must have felt unbearable. She was tired but hated leaving off on this sad part of her parents' lives, so she pushed on with the reading.

July ninth, eighteen hundred eighty-four,

I met with the women's group early today and had to tell them of the loss. I couldn't keep my excitement in at the last meeting and told them we were expecting. They were all warm and comforting. A few even attempted to reassure me that losing babes was very common and it didn't mean anything was wrong. They don't know about the first before, though, and I keep thinking I'm a failure, the problem. I feel so bad for Allen. Both times telling him, I could see the hope and excitement in his eyes. He longs to be a father and I keep failing. He isn't ready to lose hope and says I shouldn't either. I told the women of my version of the embroidery patch and they have encouraged me to still make one for this babe. They think it might be therapeutic for me. I have decided that is something I can do for my lost children and will move ahead with this project. Since the first was due in summer and this second would have come at the end of fall I have decided to make season squares.

That meant that two of those handful of squares were accounted for, but Allie was still curious to know if the others were made up ahead of time like Pa said or each one was for a special baby that never came.

Allie looked down at the squares and noted the winter and summer ones. There were two winter ones and three summer ones made up. One fall and two springs she set aside. Allie stared at the ones in front of her wondering which ones were for those two children. She felt sad looking at the squares and hoped that the making of them gave her ma some closure and comfort. She laid back down and read on.

July twenty first, eighteen hundred eighty-four,

Allen packed a picnic lunch and took me to the river. I have been so melancholy, and I think he was trying to find a way to cheer me up. It was very sweet of him. Work has him away for periods of time, and the time we do have together is short. We make the most of what we have and long for more when he is gone. I know I will pull out of this sadness at some point. Losing one was hard but losing the second just about broke me. I need to learn how to guard my heart for the future.

Allie was sad to read that. She knew her ma was tough, but she never thought that characteristic may have come from deep sadness. She always assumed it just came from living as a farmer's wife in the rugged Montana countryside. Thinking that made Allie realize she had no idea how her pa came to be a farmer. According to the journal, he was working on the railroad in the early years of their marriage.

Allie had never known about his work with the railroad before reading. She had always known him as a farmer. There was so much yet to learn about her parents and she just hoped that her ma had written it all down. She was too tired to continue on for the day, so she tucked the squares away back under the bed and put the journal on the desk before slipping back under the covers and letting sleep carry her away.

CHAPTER 35

Frank had arrived home late that night. He had worked all afternoon and into the evening on the reservation. So much was left to do, and he knew he needed to pack a bag and stay there for a while. He also knew that Allie needed him at home, which was why he didn't stay this first night. He knew he needed to get home and make sure she was and would be fine while he was away for an extended period of time. While home, he would assemble all necessary supplies to take along with him.

The house was quiet when he entered, and before going up to see Allie he rummaged through the kitchen to find a sandwich made and left for him. He gobbled it down and would properly thank Allie for thinking of him in a bit.

He ladled some of the pre-boiled water for the morning's garden into a mug and took a long swallow. The Indians didn't know and didn't practice boiling water. He refused to drink all evening and was quite parched. Making a mental note to pack some water with him when he left tomorrow, he cleaned up his supper and made his way up to

Allie.

He found Allie sound asleep and decided he didn't want to disturb her. They could talk in the morning. He made himself comfortable and gently, so not to wake her, he crawled into bed. He was successful, and Allie continued to sleep. Frank found falling asleep easy after the work from the day.

Allie woke the next morning looking at her husband. She didn't know when he'd gotten home but was happy to see him beside her. She decided to let him sleep and went downstairs to prepare breakfast. She began frying up some bacon and knew once that smell made it upstairs he would be up and ready to eat. The smell of bacon cooking could bring him home from a mile away.

Just as she assumed, Frank made his way down and wrapped his arms around her middle while she was cooking. It didn't take long for him to release her and step back, though, rubbing his arms where the bacon grease splattered on them.

Allie grabbed a towel to wipe off his arms, "I'm sorry. Are you all right?"

"Yes, I'll be fine. Bacon is one food that does find a way to get back at you for eating it."

They both laughed at that. Allie went back to cooking and Frank grabbed a cup of coffee and sat at the table.

"I didn't hear you come in last night. I was tired," Allie commented as she continued cooking.

"It's ok, I was pretty late," he said through sips.

"How did it go?"

Frank sighed. "Not good. There are a few with Typhoid and some, I think, it's too late for help. I should have stayed, but I wanted to get back to you. I had to make sure you were alright."

Allie turned to face him, mouth agape, "You shouldn't have. Frank if they need a doctor, you should go. Don't worry about me. I'll be fine here."

Frank grinned, walked to her, and gave her a long, strong hug.

"Allie, I love you. I'm planning on heading out after breakfast. I'll be gone for a while and don't know when I'll be able to return. That's why I came home last night. I wanted to let you know before I just up and disappeared on you."

"I do appreciate that, but I would have assumed duty called if you didn't return."

Allie plated the bacon and Frank snatched a piece before the plate made it to the table. She quickly fried four eggs and placed those with the plate of bacon that appeared to have more pieces gone from it.

"Would you like some eggs with your bacon dear?"

Frank grinned at her, "Yes, please."

Allie rolled her eyes at him, to which he then made sure to say thank you.

She sat down and plated her own breakfast, making sure to

take more bacon than she thought she wanted. She didn't need to finish it, but if she didn't take it now, she might not have the opportunity when she would be ready.

"I can't let you leave without providing some provisions to take with you."

Frank took a sip of coffee to help swallow his bite.

"Thanks, yes. I thought a bit about that. They haven't been boiling water. I was hoping I could take some with me."

"Of course, you can. And I have a few other things made up that I can send. I can make more for myself."

Frank finished and wiped his mouth.

"You don't need to do that. I'm sure I'll figure out something. Sister will be with me. Maybe she can help in that regard."

Allie shook her head.

"Nonsense. It's not a big deal to do that. Why don't you get a start on watering the garden for me while I put some things together?"

"Sure thing. I'll get on that right now."

"Thank you and I'll start preparing your things."

Frank kissed her forehead and made his way outside carrying the first bowl of water. The garden was small, but Allie was faithful with the watering. He could see that all the plants were strong and healthy instead of withered and brown like some of the native vegetation.

Soon canning season would come, and Frank remembered how much work that was when his ma did it. He didn't want Allie having that task all by herself. He figured by the looks of the vegetables they had a few weeks yet, and he was thankful the timing of him being away would work out, so he could help. He ran back in quickly to return the empty bowl and grab the next. Allie had already begun packing a basket.

"I'll grab the pot and fill it from the well, so you can start boiling, too."

"Okay, thanks, but I won't boil until tonight. I need to let that fire die down for now. If I try to do that after already cooking breakfast this house will be so hot, I'll need to sleep outside this afternoon."

Frank's brows drew together. "This afternoon? Are you still taking regular naps?"

Allie cringed inside. She didn't want Frank to worry about her. He had enough on his hands. "Yes, but I'm ok. I really am feeling better. The exhaustion has continued, but I'm not as weepy lately. I really think I'm getting better and with some time, this will improve, too."

Frank put his hand on her cheek. "You're sure? You don't feel sick anywhere?"

Allie nodded. "Positive."

"I hate to leave you when you aren't your full self yet. Are you sure you'll be fine?"

Allie put her hand flat on his chest and gave him a gentle shove.

"I am fine. You do what you need to do and I'll be here waiting when you have saved the day and all their lives."

Frank closed his eyes. "I'm not so sure I'll be saving all their lives, but maybe I can save a few."

"Then you must go. I'll finish up in here and you finish up out there and then you can be on your way." Allie kept a smile on her face, though she felt lonely every time he left.

Frank set his bowl down and hugged Allie tight. "I love you so."

Allie wiped a tear trailing down her cheek and onto his shoulder. "I love you, too. Now, back to work, or you'll never get out of here."

"Yes, ma'am," Frank agreed and picked up the bowl and continued with his work.

He was saying his last goodbyes and headed to his wagon less than an hour later. Allie watched him go before heading back inside to start on her chores. Having the watering completed for the day was a big burden lifted from her shoulders, and that meant she would have more reading time later. She just hoped as she read more that she would see that her parents' lives turned for the better.

Knowing that she was the oldest and was only reading about the year eighty-four, she feared there was more disappointment ahead, though.

CHAPTER 36

Frank drove the wagon back the way he came. Sister stayed on the reservation over night and was following Frank's instructions on how to care for the typhoid patients. The reservation was huge, and Frank knew he was only visiting a very small portion of it. He hoped that didn't mean that there were other groups scattered around just as sick. Frank stopped at the first house where they had begun yesterday.

The house itself was made of earth. Part had been dug away and dirt had been mounded up to make the home. Frank did see the genius in this knowing that the dirt would help keep the house cool in the summer and warm in the winter. A family group lived here. There was a grandmother, the parents, and a few little kids. Not speaking the language and only relying on Sister meant he didn't have much information. He knew the basics and that was enough for now.

Sister greeted him as he climbed down from the wagon. She looked tired.

"I assumed you would stop here first on your way

through, so I made my rounds making this my last stop during the night."

"How are they doing? You must be exhausted." Frank grabbed his bag off the seat and together they started walking to the entrance.

"Not well. I did try to educate them on boiling water. A few agreed to try it, but others think it will kill the life in the water."

"It's supposed to. Any bacteria growing should be dead in the process so it doesn't infect people."

"I understand this, but they view water as sacred and as life itself. They don't want to kill that."

"Well, then, we have our work cut out for us, don't we?"

Frank looked at Sister and she nodded back. It would be tough to convince them to trust his direction when it went against their beliefs. It would be like Frank or Sister being told to quit going to church because the building was haunted by death.

They walked through the opening and Frank blinked a few times as his eyes adjusted to the dim light. Then he nodded at a couple of people standing looking at him before making his way to the little boy who lay on the bed.

He was not looking good and Frank feared it was too late. He spoke to Sister as he examined the boy, and Sister relayed the information to the adults standing by. Unfortunately, it sounded as though this boy was not only suffering from typhoid, but pneumonia had set in as well. Based on the size of him, he had to be somewhere around five years of age. Watching a child die was one of the hardest parts of his job. He gave the boy what he could to ease his suffering and explained to Sister that they should focus on those who fared better.

Frank wasn't sure what sister translated, but based on the crying and moans coming from the woman he knew she must have told them death was imminent. Frank looked at them feeling helpless. It was in such times as this that he hated his profession.

He stepped back out into the sun, shielding his eyes from the brightness. Sister came out shortly after he did, and they solemnly climbed into the wagon to head to the next house. The day was just beginning and already it was looking to be a long one.

They arrived at the next earth house and fortunately, this home seemed to be doing well and Frank would take that good news. He instructed sister to pass along the water boiling need and they continued to the next home.

After traveling for a while and seeing to the needs of a few here and there with minor ailments, they came to another house that had typhoid. This was a woman who looked to be a bit older than Frank, but still in her prime. A male appeared to be in the early stages of sickness as well. Frank quickly assessed the two and got to work.

Luckily this home took the need to boil water to heart and they already had some going. The woman was in bed and looked to be in as poor of shape as the first boy they saw. The man was up trying to fend for her.

Frank assumed they were a couple by the looks of things. He ordered the man to bed, and Sister took over what he was tending to. He administered what medication he could and started forcing water into them. Hydration was key to helping offset the fever and other messier portions of the disease. Once he had done all he could, he instructed Sister on how to keep the fevers down manually and decided to continue onward leaving Sister behind to care for their needs. He needed to get to more homes to make sure he was doing all he could for everyone.

Without his interpreter, Frank soon discovered not everyone was eager to welcome him in. Plus, not being able to communicate in any capacity was frustrating. He did what he could and assessed the homes of those who would allow him. He did find a few more people in the early typhoid stages and they were willing to let him treat them. It took longer than he liked trying to convey that it would be easier if they could all be together to be treated. A few of the kids helped with translating what they could since they were in school learning English. Frank included a silent thanks to God for that in his frequent prayers. It was something he now did as he entered and left each home.

Organization was needed for efficiency. Frank brought the patients by wagon to the largest of the homes where blankets were laid on the floor for padding for each. He could not convince the healthy to stay away so he could properly quarantine the area. No one trusted him enough to leave him alone with their sick. The white doctor was not their Medicine Man. He could understand that as a husband. He wouldn't leave anyone alone with Allie if she was sick, certainly not an outsider he had just met. He supposed he couldn't ask these people to do what he himself wouldn't be comfortable with as well.

Once everyone was settled, he put water on to boil. It would be a while before he could start serving it as it needed to fully cool, so it wouldn't burn them going down. Once that was set, he began showing those who stayed how to help keep them cool and comfortable. If they chose to stay, they might as well be useful, Frank thought. Teaching them would then allow him to travel between the two typhoid homes to keep up on the progress of both. The children proved to be a bigger asset than he first thought. They not only could help translate, but they were quick to learn.

Frank continued with his first day going back and forth teaching as he went. By nightfall he was exhausted but knew he couldn't get sleep with his two sickest patients needing around the clock care. He decided to attempt to split up those who stayed at the second home to help with the first. This way they all could take turns sleeping. It was the same approach he took before. This time around there were many more hands making the work load lighter and the time to sleep longer. He wasn't sure how long he would need to be here and hoped he could get back to Allie soon. He knew it would be several days at least with what he had so far. He prayed no one else fell ill to typhoid.

CHAPTER 37

Allie woke the next morning and began her chores. She was determined to get them all done while the weather was bearable. She also decided to start napping in the living room, as the bedroom heat was stifling on the second story of their home.

With the watering for the day behind her, she went back inside and began on the inside chores. Allie had packed all the bread she had made up for Frank. More would need baked, but she dreaded the thought of the added heat that would bring. Deciding to begin that later in the day so it would be ready for baking at the same time she was boiling water, she moved into Frank's office.

Normally, it was in use during the day and Allie couldn't get in to give it a good cleaning. Since Frank was gone, this was her opportunity to do just that. She wasn't in there all of five minutes when a knock sounded on the front door. Allie was glad it wasn't an office door knock. She wasn't sure what she would do if a true emergency came in when he was gone.

She made her way to the front door as the second knock came. Pulling the door open her eyes grew round with surprise.

"Oh, Emma, Roger, kids... what a lovely surprise."

"Hi, Allie," Roger spoke first, and Emma gave Allie a hug.

"Come in, come in," Allie moved aside so they could file in. She tousled Alex's hair. "Well, get a look at you. You look all healed and mighty strong. I'm so glad."

Alex grew sheepish and wrapped an arm around his father's leg.

"Since when did you become afraid of me?" Allie turned to look at Emma who had grown rounder since she had seen her last.

Emma put her hand on her stomach in acknowledgment.

"He just started doing that. He has never been shy, but now he won't talk to anyone."

"Well, that's okay," she looked down at Alex who was now peeking out behind Roger's leg.

"I don't have anything here to serve you. Frank headed to the reservation and he took all my baked goods with him," Allie put her knuckles on her mouth mentally going through what she had on hand to see if anything would be suitable.

"Oh, not to worry Allie, we aren't staying. I'm just dropping off Roger and supplies. Then I'll drive the wagon and children back home for the day." Emma and Roger smiled at each other.

"Roger and supplies?" Allie was confused.

Roger picked up Alex. "Yes ma'am, I will never be able to repay your husband for what he did for us, but I can build you a chicken coop and start your flock."

Allie was silent processing what he just said. "You don't need to do all that. That's his job."

Roger passed Alex to Emma.

"Yes, it is his job and being a job, it comes with a fee. He went above and beyond to save my little boy and I wanted to do something above and beyond for him. Now, I'll go unload the wagon and it will be ready for you," he looked at Emma and added, "in a couple of minutes." Roger stepped outside and unloaded all the wood and nails. The ladies and children stepped out onto the porch and waited.

Emma set Alex down and grabbed Allie's hand.

"I'm going to come pick Roger up later today and when I do, I will bring the birds."

Allie smiled. "It's going to be wonderful having eggs right here that I don't need to regularly purchase. I can't thank you both enough."

"No thanks needed," Emma grabbed Alex's hand and led him off the porch as Katie followed behind her. Roger lifted his children up into the wagon and then helped Emma climb up. They all waved as they drove off, leaving Allie and Roger on the front lawn.

"Now, where would you like this to go?" Roger turned to Allie and waited.

Allie put her hands on her hips. "Well now, I'm not sure." She scanned around thinking. "I know I'll want it in the back. Maybe the far side away from the office?"

Roger thought that was a good idea. They walked around back and quickly found a suitable spot. He moved his supplies and got to work. Allie watched for a little while before she made her way back inside to finish her chores.

Allie went back out in the middle of the day with a tall glass of boiled water. She handed it to Roger and checked on the progress. "I can find something to eat for you if you're hungry."

Roger took the glass and downed half of it. "No, thanks. Emma packed me a lunch, but this water is hitting the spot. Thanks, though."

Allie walked over to the structure. Roger had all four sides already on and was working on the roof.

"I'm going to have a chicken ladder with the opening in the floor. That way in the winter time, the cold winds won't blow through the side."

Allie looked back at Roger. "That sounds like a great idea. You've made great progress already."

Roger wiped his brow. "I'll be done here in the next couple of hours. Once this is done I'm going to walk over to the livery and pick up some of their hay for the bedding."

"Well, do you need anything else?" Allie took the glass Roger handed back to her.

"I could use some more of this water in a bit. It's a warm one today."

"Will do," Allie turned to leave and swayed on her feet for a moment. Roger grabbed her waist and steadied her.

"Are you all right?"

Allie blinked. "I think I'm fine now. I was a little dizzy for a moment, but I already feel better."

Roger looked at her. "Let me help you inside. Maybe you just are too warm."

Together they made their way in and Roger helped her sit. "I'm going to go get you a glass of water. Then if you're still feeling fine I'll head back out to work."

"Water sounds lovely. It is miserably hot."

Allie took the water from Roger and drank several gulps. "That is exactly what I needed. Thank you. I'm feeling much better now."

"Good. I'll head back out. You stay in here away from the sun. Let me know if you need anything. You know where I'll be, and I will let you know before I go get that hay."

Allie nodded. She wasn't sure what that dizzy spell was about but decided she should stay in and rest a bit. After Roger headed back out, she went upstairs to grab the journal and back down to the living room to read. Before she settled in, she made sure her water was filled up and sitting on the little table next to her. She opened the journal and began reading her ma's words and she listened to the pounding of hammer on nails outside.

CHAPTER 38

Allie woke each morning to the sound of a rooster. Roger had finished the coop a few days back and Emma brought three young red hens and a proud red rooster with green tail feathers with her when she returned for him. That noise was something she would need to get used to. He was loud.

She had restocked the baking since Frank's departure. Today was quilting day and she was happy to be able to sit with some friends. Being alone gave her lots of reading time and she was sad to learn that her parents suffered more loss.

Allie had read of the loss of another four children, leaving only two squares unaccounted for. She knew by the pattern that they would be claimed when she read more. She was getting closer to her birth, so she wasn't sure if all the loss came before her or if there was at least one between her and Drew. She wasn't sure she wanted to know the answer to that question.

Allie also discovered how her pa became a farmer and

she loved him all the more for it. They had both suffered so much loss and her ma was struggling with depression. Pa decided that his life of being gone for days and sometimes weeks at a time was more than Ma could deal with, so he up and quit.

Time was shaky for a bit. He took what he had saved up and bought the farm. Money was a struggle from then on, but they managed, and the depression seemed to ease based on her writing. Allie had mixed feelings about learning all this information. She loved feeling like she still had a connection to her ma, but she hated knowing what they went though.

Allie entered and saw that some of the other women had already begun working on their current blanket. Emma and Belle looked up at her. Both stood and greeted her before they all took their seats. Everyone made small talk. They would finish this blanket today. Some of the ladies had brought treats and she could see a pitcher of what looked like apple cider.

Allie joined in working after she settled in. Both Emma and Belle were awfully quiet. Too quiet. Normally the three of them carried on their own conversation, but today the silent air hung over Allie and it made her nervous. Something was going on with them and Allie had not a clue what it could be. One of the women spoke up, breaking the silence that hung at one end of the table.

"I heard Dr. Hubbard was helping the Indians."

All eyes looked at Allie which only made her uneasiness worsen. "Yes, he has been there for several days now. He told me there were a few typhoid cases."

That started mini conversations all around the table. Some women were mentioning praying for them, others were talking about the Indians as savages and Dr. Hubbard shouldn't waste his time on them.

Belle's voice rose above the others. "I, for one, am happy to hear he is helping. Doc Hubbard and Allie have been a wonderful addition to our community and I thank them for all their hard work." She looked at Allie and if Allie could have had the floor open up and swallow her whole she would have welcomed that.

"Thank you, Belle," Allie whispered the words and stared down at her work.

The rest of the women carried on with their small group conversations around the table and Allie silently worked. Some of the women had finished their portions and were now up mingling and enjoying the refreshments. Allie felt a tap on her shoulder and Emma was there holding a glass of cider out for her.

"Roger told me you had a dizzy spell the other day. How are you feeling now?"

Allie stood and took the glass from her. She stepped away from the table so if any cider spilt it wouldn't get on the quilt. "I did, but I'm feeling fine now."

"Really? No other symptoms?" Emma was looking her over.

Allie started fidgeting. "Well, I've been tired. Frank says it's all normal for the grieving process. And I think the dizzy was from being in the direct sun in the middle of the day." Allie felt someone behind her and turned to see Belle there.

Both women looked at each other. Emma spoke, "Yes, well, if Frank said that, I'm sure he is right."

"Right, my ear," Belle all but shouted out. She lowered her voice for the next part. "Allie dear, I believe you may be pregnant."

Allie was shocked and too stunned to speak. She set her cider down and looked around the room.

"Thank you all for the wonderful treats. I'm sorry I can't stay to finish." She fled the room and once outside began running. Emma and Belle followed after her.

"Allie, wait. Come back," they both insisted.

Allie headed to the creek and didn't slow until she was standing on the banks edge. Belle and Emma were a bit slower given one was much older and the other increasing in size. They stopped, both a bit out of breath when they caught up with her.

"I'm sorry to have upset you, Allie, I was just concerned. After Roger..."

Allie interrupted Emma. "You have no idea." She looked at Emma first and then turned to Belle. "When you said that, I panicked. I haven't let much of my past known in these regards. It can't be, and it's just got me so confused. First, my long-time doctor had to do a procedure to help my body with a miscarriage from my first husband, then he said my chances of getting pregnant again were slim to none. Now, I am married to a doctor who knows about everything, but the dizziness and he says I'm just grieving."

Allie wasn't going to add the fact she now knew her ma's history of miscarriages. If Allie did somehow manage to get pregnant, the likelihood of keeping it to term was dismal. She didn't even want to think about losing another and tears sprang to her eyes thinking of how many times her ma went through it.

"Oh, Allie, I'm sorry," Emma put her hand on Allie's back. "I'm sure Frank is right. I'm no doctor and shouldn't act at all like one."

Belle crossed her arms over her chest. "Well, I'm not. You are pregnant, and I know it for a fact. I can see it on you."

Both Emma and Allie stared agape at Belle who was now storming off in the direction from which they came. "I'm sorry she said that. I don't know why she would after what you said to us." Emma was trying to comfort her.

Allie took a deep breath. "It's ok. She is entitled to her opinion and that's all that is."

She really wanted to stay here alone and sit at the water, but she needed Emma to leave so instead she told Emma she wanted to head home. She made up a story about some work that she had left undone before joining the other women to work on the quilt and she wanted to finish it. Emma and Allie walked back as far as they could together and then both parted to head separate ways.

All that talk threw Allie into a panic. She was rapidly trying to remember back to her last menses and was struggling to come up with a definite date. Since her ma died, life was all a blur. She had specific moments that stood out to her marking time passing, but the usual day to day stuff all blended together. She couldn't remember the last one and that frightened her.

Allie realized she would rather not ever be pregnant then have to live with being scared every day wondering if this was the last day her child would live. She marched in her house and grabbed the journal. She decided she would read up until she was born. Allie knew her ma had two successful pregnancies, obviously, but she needed to read it and see how her ma got through each day of those. If Belle was right she would need all the strength she could to not go mad with worry.

She wasn't ready to agree with Belle, but she knew that both pregnancy and grief could explain her symptoms. She would wait and let Frank decide. Waiting for him to get home would make her just as anxious.

CHAPTER 39

Allie had read through the night and was sound asleep when a pounding woke her with a jolt. She wiped the sleep out of her eyes and stood up from the chair in the living room she had fallen asleep in the night before. Ma's journal dropped to the floor from her lap. Allie quickly picked it up and rushed to the front door.

When she opened it no one was there, but the pounding continued. She turned back and headed to Frank's office. Feeling a sense of dread and worry about what or who she might find, she twisted the handle and pulled the door open.

A man was standing on the other side with his fist in the air ready to pound again.

"I'm sorry ma'am," he was wincing in pain and his right arm hung at an odd angle.

"Please, please come in." Allie stepped aside so he could

enter.

"Is Doc in ma'am?" He was hopping back and forth.

Allie suggested he sit. "I'm sorry, but Doctor Hubbard is away today. Can I help you?" She had no idea what she was doing, but this man was in pain and she couldn't let him leave without any aid.

"Oh, I can come back ma'am," he stood attempting to leave.

Allie stood as well and blocked his exit. "Nonsense. I'm not the doctor, but I have helped him enough times that I'm sure I can do something for you." She lied, but she wanted to reassure him somehow.

"Well, okay," he sat back down.

"Good. Now, tell me who you are and what happened." She began feeling his head for fever and looking him over as best as she could.

"Sam, name's Sam. I was on a ladder picking apples and my step broke. I fell and landed wrong on my elbow."

"Ouch, I bet that hurts. Do you have any other injuries?"

"No, just some bruising here and there."

Allie stood next to his right side and bent over a bit to get a better view. "That's good Sam. One injury is always more than enough. Can you move it?"

Sam worked at moving any part of his arm, but it all hurt. He could not bend his elbow. His wrist and fingers still had movement, but it pained him to try. Allie thought for a while as she scanned the room for inspiration. Seeing some towels, she sparked an idea.

"Sam, I am going to stabilize your arm. It won't fix it, but maybe we can reduce some pain while you wait to see Fra...Dr. Hubbard."

He nodded.

"Good. Let's get your arm against your body so I can wrap this towel around your arm and tie it to you.

Sam moved his arm from his shoulder and positioned it across his stomach grimacing in pain through the whole move. Allie cradled his arm in the towel and brought the ends up to tie around his neck.

Immediately Sam's face unclenched.

"Thank you. It still hurts real bad, but the towel is holding my arm up so I don't have to do that myself. It feels a little better." Sam slumped with some relief, but still in visible discomfort.

Allie smiled and took a deep breath. "I'm glad. I wish I could do more for you, but we are both going to need to wait for Dr. Hubbard to get back. I'm not sure when that will be, either, I'm afraid. He is on the reservation treating the Indians. I'm sure the doctor in North Yakima will be happy to treat you, though, if you can't wait."

Sam stood. "That's all right. I'll give him a day and if he hasn't gotten back, I'll head north. I'm not sure how I will sleep tonight, but one night I will make due. Thank you."

She was grinning at her accomplishment. "Thank you. It's not every day that I get to take over my husband's job."

Sam headed out the door and Allie closed it gently and twisted the lock. She made her way across the office to Frank's desk. She needed to find suitable material to write out notes for Frank. She wanted to remember each detail to share with him. If she waited, she ran the risk of forgetting. She hoped he came home soon. Sam was in great pain and Frank would be better able to help with that. Allie had been nervous and worked to make sure Sam hadn't known. Frank was level headed in an emergency. He always maintained his calmness and evenness. Allie loved that about him as a doctor and a husband.

Allie started on the chores. Her energy was waning and she was becoming quite sleepy again. She knew she needed to get the watering done or they would go without today. As she was working, her thoughts kept going back to her parents' early years.

They'd suffered so much loss and disappointment, yet they grew closer and their faith stronger. Instead of blaming the other they made choices to get closer. They regularly worked together to find things to do.

Pa's choice in changing his job meant they were available to each other every day. Ma chose to work side by side with Pa instead of allowing the depression to take hold and swallow her whole. Allie always knew her parents held a great strength within them, but she didn't know how deep that ran until now.

She paused between watering by the new coop and watched the chickens. They were oblivious to her standing there. They went about their daily business without a care in the world. Allie realized then that she held bitterness in her heart. Eddie's choice and actions still controlled her. She still felt powerless.

She wasn't fearful anymore, but she was still angry. Eddie still controlled her emotions. The loss of her first child's blame was always placed on Eddie, but knowing now her parents' struggles, maybe that baby would have been lost regardless of the abuse. Maybe nothing could have changed that outcome.

Allie had beat herself up for making that first choice of marrying Eddie. If she hadn't, she always thought she wouldn't have suffered that great loss. She now understood that it had to happen the way it did. That choice led to her present. She and Frank may have never rediscovered interest in each other after so long. She had learned that she needed to wait and follow God's plan, but she was just fully understanding that when you didn't, He still found a way to make good in the bad. Sometimes it wasn't easy to see, but it was there. And following God's plan isn't always visible, as so many necessary events seem so mundane or unfavorable.

Allie retrieved more boiled water and continued her watering. She read the happiness that her parents shared through the pain. Her ma moved past being fearful of another failed pregnancy to just enjoying what she had.

Reading the transformation of her ma, she herself began to transform as well. Allie was no longer afraid of the possibility of being pregnant. She knew that God held her and this baby, if there was one, in His hands. If she was to become a mother, it would be in His time and not a moment sooner.

Allie silently gave thanks to God for allowing her this knowledge and comfort. She hated that her ma died, but without that she wouldn't have learned about her parents' journey, and through them saw her own ugliness that still lived within her.

She set down her bowl and bent on her knees. In that moment she spoke to God, forgave Eddie for the atrocities he did to her, and released her first child from her heart and fully to God. She would no longer fear the future and what it may hold but love what she had and work to come closer to God. Now, with letting go of the hatred for Eddie, she could focus on her love for Frank. If her parents could learn to do that with everything that happened to them, she could as well.

Allie felt lighter when she stood up. Everything that she had been feeling since her ma passed wasn't weighing as heavily on her. She wondered if she was grieving more or feeling it longer for her ma due to holding anger in her heart before that.

She knew that changing this would be a daily choice. Giving this to God once was a good start, but each day she would need to reaffirm her choice of letting God guide her and not hold on to the hate. Love was harder and more elusive. Hate came easily. She knew she would have her ups and downs. Some days would be easier than others, but from this day on she would wake making the conscious choice to love even the unlovable.

CHAPTER 40

Frank was exhausted. Even though he set up around the clock care that allowed him time to rest, he could never really rest. They lost two but were able to save the others. Those that died were a five-year-old little boy and a woman in her late thirties. He would never get use to the times when he lost patients and he didn't want to. Some doctors just carried on like nothing happened, but each loss effected Frank deeply on the inside, though he tried to remain professional on the exterior.

Today, Frank could finally go back home. Everything that he could do had been done. He left instructions on prevention and what to do should any symptoms crop up with new patients. Even though he was deeply tired, he decided to first head to North Yakima and meet with Dr. Henry Green. Frank wanted to update him on the typhoid cases south of the city.

Penny pulled Frank's wagon into the hustle and bustle of North Yakima and he directed her through and around the chaos of city life. He could tell that the push for a cleaner city was not all falling on deaf ears. The streets were cleaner. The pungent smell of the dairy farms still hung heavy in the air, though. He steered Penny through each turn and block after block through the city until Henry's office was in sight. It did appear that Henry was in as he brought the wagon to a stop in front of the office.

He set the brake and gave Penny a neck pat before entering the dimly lit sitting area. The bell on the door jingled with its closing. Henry called from the back to have a seat and he would be right with him. Frank started to call out and then refrained, realizing that he could have a patient with him. He sat and waited and allowed his eyes time to adjust to the lighting.

Henry came out and instantly smiled when he saw who was waiting.

"Ah, Frank. I'm glad you stopped in. I've been meaning to catch up with you."

Frank rose. "I've been on the reservation for the last several days."

"Really? What took you out that way?"

Frank sighed. "Typhoid. I was just on my way back home but decided to delay and see you first to give you an update."

"I see. Well, my boy, I have some information to pass along to you on the subject as well." Henry sat in one of the chairs and motioned for Frank to also.

He took the seat next to Henry before updating him on the handful of cases and the two deaths. Henry retrieved one of his notebooks to note the deaths before returning to his seat.

"They do have their own way of treating and handling illness and ailments. We do see them head this way occasionally for our help, though."

Frank agreed they did have their own approach and he was thankful many listened to him on what needed done in this instance.

"While I was there treating the typhoid, I did see some other things, too. I pulled a few teeth in an elderly man. We couldn't communicate, but after the initial pain of pulling the teeth he jumped up and down laughing and hugging me. I knew he was very thankful and happy I could help him." Frank smiled at the memory.

"Yes, they are mostly a peaceful group and the ones I have encountered I have enjoyed."

"So, how is the typhoid epidemic developing here?" Frank was ready to head home to Allie but wanted an update first.

"I'm glad you asked. That was why I wanted to talk with you, actually. While we are still treating new cases, Mr. Lumsden has found one of the sources. Now, I say one because any water source that gets contaminated could develop into typhoid. Same as if using that water to grow food or just simply the plants getting their own contaminated water pulled up through their roots. Water must still be boiled, but the number of cases we have been seeing should recede."

Frank was listening intently. "That is great news. So, what was it?"

Henry folded his arms and cleared his throat a bit.

"Well, that answer is a bit disgusting. Seems the Cascade Lumber Company's privies overhang a canal that connected to a pond that dumps into the river. Now, there is supposed to be a valve that closes that off or something to that nature, but somehow that valve opened up. No one knows if this was intentional, given the low water level this time of year, or if it was accidentally switched. Regardless, human waste had made its way into our drinking water. It's a wonder more people didn't get sick. I am thankful for the knowledge to boil the water. And, that many have listened and taken up that practice."

Frank was visibly disgusted. "Well, maybe now that the main source has been identified more people will understand the need to boil the water. Until we can come up with a sanitation process at the city level, every citizen must do what they can to ensure their own health."

"I agree." Henry folded his hands as though in prayer and looked for a moment to the heavens. Then made his way to the door and opened it causing the little bell to sound.

"I'll keep doing what I can on my end and let's hope the worst of it is truly behind us." Frank said as he made his way through the open door and Henry followed him out.

"Thanks for the report from the reservation. I'll continue here stressing our recommendations." He wiped his nose. "Maybe I'll start campaigning for the dairies to be relocated as well. Not only are they a possible source for future typhoid, they flat out stink."

Frank chuckled. "That they do. I'm going to head back out to my place in the country side where we have fresh air."

Both men laughed. Frank hopped up and released the brake before urging Penny forward. He was now on his way home he hoped for a good long while. Being apart from Allie was always hard, but reuniting was easy. He prayed she was still moving forward. Losing her ma seemed harder on her than going through the previous year of dealing with Eddie. He wasn't sure how to help her, but at least he could be home for a time now to figure it out.

CHAPTER 41

Frank pulled up to the livery and parked his wagon before unhitching Penny and leading her to her stall. He brushed her down while she ate some grain. She had worked hard while they were gone, and Frank thought she would be happy resting up and being pampered a bit. Once finished, he was able to walk the rest of the way home.

The closer he got to the house, he could hear singing. It took him until he reached the fence to realize it was Allie and it was coming from the back of the house. Frank broke into a grin and bypassed the front door to meet her out back. He froze in his tracks when he saw who she was singing to.

Her back was to him and she hadn't realized yet that he was there. They had birds, chickens to be exact, and a coop. Frank was shocked and curious to know how those got there. He didn't think Allie could have done that herself, although it wouldn't be the first time she would have surprised him with her abilities. This was a little more than he thought her capable of, though. Alone, anyway.

He decided not to scare her and made his presence known instead of just silently approaching. She squealed in delight and he lifted her off the ground twirling her as they hugged.

"Frank!" Allie shouted before smothering him in kisses.

"Oh, Allie, you are a sight for sore, tired eyes."

He set her down and stood back to look at her. She was stunning. Then he looked back at the chickens, which made Allie chuckle.

"I bet you're wondering where these lovelies came from." Allie picked up a nearby basket with two brown eggs inside and held it for Frank to see.

"Well, yes, although I wouldn't call them lovelies myself," Frank raised one brow and looked back at her.

"Oh, I didn't at first either, but they are growing on me. These fresh daily eggs are wonderful."

"So, how did they find their way to our back yard?"

"Payment." Allie nodded her head once.

Frank was confused. "Payment for what?"

She looked squarely at him, "For you, silly. Roger came by several days ago and built this coop. Then later that day Emma brought the chickens with her. It is their way of saying thank you for helping them with Alex."

"Oh," dawning washed over his face. "I suppose Roger had hinted at such. I should have taken him seriously. They didn't need to do that, though."

"I know and told them just that, but they really wanted to and fresh eggs straight from our yard is nice so..." Allie grabbed his hand and led him back to the house. "Tell me about the Indians."

Frank didn't want to bring her happy mood down, but there was no way around not telling her about the deaths... one a child, no less. She was saddened to hear about it, but it didn't permanently sour her mood like he thought it might. When he left, she was still battling her ever changing mood swings.

"You seem better. How are you feeling?"

"I am. I've had a lot of time on my hands and have read much. My ma has helped me through her journal."

Frank was happy to hear this and hoped this was the beginning of a permanent change and not just for today.

"Oh, Frank, before I forget. Follow me." She grabbed his hand again and led him to his office where she handed him some notes.

He studied them. "You treated a patient?"

Allie paused a moment, not sure if he was happy or angry with her or if treatment was truly what she provided.

"Well kind of. I just immobilized his arm so further damage couldn't be done. I didn't administer medications or anything like that. I think it's broken, but I didn't tell him that. I wasn't wanting to worry him in case I was wrong."

Frank looked back down over the notes.

"You did a fantastic job. I may have you sit in from time to time to learn more. We never know when I'll be called away again and you might have something literally fall on the doorstep that can't wait. Things like this. I wouldn't have or expect you to treat a patient, but providing some comfort, assessing the situation, and basic care could be beneficial for many."

Allie was relieved to hear that he wasn't upset with her. She was also proud to know that she didn't do something wrong with Sam. She may have not helped him get better, but she didn't make him worse.

"So, tell me more about what happened around here when I was away. Treating a patient and acquiring chickens are a couple of big things. Anything else of importance?"

So much happened when he was gone, but Allie wasn't sure how to put her thoughts and feelings into words. "I said before I read. I learned a lot through that. Not only about my parents, but also about myself."

Frank liked the sound of where this was headed. It sounded like a deeper healing than time only could accomplish.

"I realized that I was still harboring anger. Anger towards Eddie about what he did to me and my child," she had turned away from him and was talking to the wall.

Frank had not expected Eddie to still be a part of the equation. She hadn't acted scared of Frank for a long time. He assumed when her behavior towards him became more trusting was when she had healed from her wounds of her first marriage. He stayed silent and let her talk.

"Do you know that my parents went through eight miscarriages? Eight, before they had me." She was speaking to him, but not looking at him. "They could have let bitterness take over, but they instead chose to love. They loved each other and God, and with each loss, after the initial couple, their love only grew. That is a level of strength I don't know I have, but if they could do that I will try."

Frank was confused. She was just talking about Eddie and her anger with him. Then she shifted to her parents, but he didn't see the clear connection she had obviously formed.

"I realized that my hurt for the loss of my baby was eating a hole clear through me. I directed my anger towards a man who has been dead and unable to do anything for close to a year now. I was able to function until I lost Ma. I wasn't whole enough to deal with that and it sent me spiraling down with my emotions. I am sad about my ma, but I have been able to put it in perspective since I was able to weed out the anger from the other. Dealing with one has allowed me to overcome the other and find the joy in having her in my life for as long as I did. Not everyone is as fortunate. And her journal is such a treasure that I will hold dear forever. I hear her voice so clearly when I read it."

Frank smiled at her. "I am so happy to hear this. I have been pretty worried about you and hated having to leave you."

Allie looked him in the eyes. "I was also worried that someday you would decide you couldn't live without children and hate me for my inability to conceive and carry. Knowing the sacrifices and changes Pa made for Ma, I realized I was adding stress and worry when there was none. You are a good man and my fears were based on my first relationship, not my current one."

Frank wrapped his arms around her in a protective hug. "I've told you before that I love you and while children would be welcome, they are not required. I do wish you would have taken me at my word, but I am thankful you found your way here in your own time."

Allie pulled back. "No. Not in my own time. In God's time. I really think I wouldn't have been ready to listen and understand the lesson before if I knew all of this. I'm not sure it would have had the same impact as it does now. Ma dying and having her journal after my first marriage, loss of my child, remarrying and moving away would have been easier to skip over and miss the message if any of these didn't fall into place as they had. I don't think God gave me all the heartache to bring me to this point, but I do think He used it and found the light within it for His work."

Frank found tears forming in his eyes as he listened to Allie speak. He took his thumb and rubbed her cheek. "So, is that all you did while I was gone?" He smiled while he said it so she would know he was teasing. Allie had gone through a transformation while he was at the reservation.

"Actually, no."

Frank was caught by surprise with that answer. He couldn't possibly imagine how she's had time for anything else but remained silent so she could continue.

"I had a dizzy spell while Roger was here building the coop. He got me inside and had me drink some water. I thought it was just the heat. Then I went to my women's group for our weekly work meeting and Belle had other ideas. I was terrified at first as she announced her opinion in the matter before I had uncovered all that I just told you."

Frank pulled back switching into doctor mode. "You were dizzy. Has this happened again?"

"A couple of times now, yes."

He ordered her up on his table and begun a thorough exam assessing head to feet. When he palpitated her abdomen, he was dumbfounded. Her uterus was larger than it should be.

"Uh, Allie."

"I'm pregnant aren't I?"

He looked at her in shock. "How did you know?"

Allie chuckled. "I didn't. Belle did."

"How did Belle know?" He still stared at her wondering how someone who only saw Allie occasionally could see what he, a doctor who lived with her, missed.

"I don't know. Maybe she was just enough outside to see what we overlooked as natural parts of grieving. I haven't had common symptoms either. I've not gotten sick and my clothing is still all fitting as normal."

"That's true. When was your last cycle?"

"I've thought on that, too. It was sometime around the time before I left for Montana, I think. I can't remember much. All that time is hazy."

"Well judging as best I can tell, you are around four months or so. That would mean this new little one should arrive sometime around Christmas."

Allie started crying and Frank was concerned she was upset. "Frank do you think I could lose this one? Ma lost so many."

Frank held her hand. "That is always a possibility, but you are past the first portion when most miscarriages happen. I think your odds of carrying to term are just as good if not better than the possible loss."

"I don't understand how. Doc was fairly sure I could never," Allie put her hand on her forehead absorbing all of this information.

"Doc is only human. He isn't all knowing and only told you what he would have told anyone given the circumstances. While what you went through does lesson the possibility, it doesn't extinguish it."

"Oh, Frank!" She sat up and kissed him on the lips. "I know just the quilt square I will use." She got up from the table and hurried into the main part of the house.

Frank was once again confused. He had no idea what she was talking about regarding a quilt square. He entered the kitchen as she came running back down the stairs.

"Now just a minute here," Frank scolded. "You will not be running on those stairs ever. Now, what has you all in a huff?"

Allie held out the square.

"Remember these? I found them under the bed after Ma passed. She made these for each of her children. Drew and I have ours in our baby blankets. Each loose one was from each of her children they lost. This one here was from her second. That child was due also around Christmas. I am going to finish this blanket and give it to our child. My second, also..." She said the last more to herself than to Frank and Allie felt bittersweet realizing that connection.

"That sounds like a fine idea, but I need you to slow down. You also need to eat more and make sure you are drinking plenty of water. I think that might have been the cause of your dizziness. I'm going to be pretty strict about all of this until we know for sure and most likely until that baby is here in my arms."

"In your arms huh?" They embraced again.

EPILOGUE

Allie wrapped Allen up in the blanket she made for him with Ma's handiwork in the center. Frank looked on, his eyes aglow, taking in the scene of mother and son. He had been born two days before Christmas and was the best present either Frank or Allie had ever received. They chose the name Allen after Allie's pa. She hoped he grew up to fill the rather large shoes of his namesake.

"Are you ready for church?" Frank donned his Sunday shoes and looked to Allie to see if she was ready.

"We are. He is all changed and bundled up. I really wish spring would hurry up and get here. I am tired of all this snow and am ready for some flowers."

"Oh, it's only March dear. You know that April showers are supposed to bring May flowers. Not March flowers." He helped her into a sweater.

"Yes, I do. I'm just being impatient is all." She swayed a

bit on her feet and Frank steadied her.

"You've been drinking your water, haven't you?" Frank spoke with a concerned look on his face.

"Of course, but really dear, I cannot imagine getting pregnant so soon after having Allen is good for my health."

"It does come with its own issues, but I know you'll do just fine," he winked at her.

"Oh, really, and how do you know that?" She looked up at him with a slight smirk on her face.

"Because I'm the doctor and I'm going to see to it that you follow doctor's orders to a T." He kissed her temple and helped her out and into the waiting wagon. They were still living in town, as he hadn't been able yet to buy the farm he wanted. Based on how fast their family was growing, they may be forced out of this house sooner than he thought. He knew he needed to find a permanent home instead of their rental. Now that his practice had grown he could change his focus and do just that.

Allie held Allen with one hand and was biting her nails on the other. "I'm not sure what to do."

Frank climbed up and turned to look at Allie. "What to do about what."

"Oh, I was talking to myself. Never mind. It's all right," she scratched her nail on her skirt attempting to file down the rough edge she'd created.

The last almost two years had brought mostly chaos. Frank wasn't sure he could deal with anymore. "Maybe I can help. What's the problem?"

"Well, Ma only had one baby due in the fall. That means I only have one square for that season. What if we have more children born then, though?"

Frank laughed. "Oh, Allie. That is a problem I hope we have." He flicked the reigns and Penny pulled the wagon forward.

A note from the author

Thank you for reading my second novel. After I wrote my first, I knew the characters were not finished telling their story. I needed a location for them to do so and came upon the typhoid epidemic in Yakima. There isn't much to be found regarding this event and even less when concerning the Natives from the area. There is no information revealing anything more other than two natives, one young and one middle aged, died from typhoid. I have no way to know if a doctor did assist them or if there were more who fell ill. I do not know if detailed notes were kept by the doctors, but it fit my story so I added it. All other details are factual. As a result of this epidemic, the way Yakima handled the situation became a model for other small and rural communities across the county.

I hope you enjoy reading it as much as I enjoyed writing it. You can leave a message or ask a question on my website stefaniebridges-mikota.wixsite.com/website, email at stefaniemikota@gmail.com, or Facebook https://www.facebook.com/Fiction.Novel.Author/. If you could take a moment and leave an Amazon review I would greatly appreciate that. I love hearing from my readers. I have begun additional works and hope to incorporate interests of my readers.

ABOUT THE AUTHOR

Stefanie Bridges-Mikota grew up in a small town in SW Washington halfway between the beautiful Pacific Ocean and majestic Cascade Mountains. She was raised by two hard working people who instilled old time values in a modern world. She married her high school sweetheart and together they have two children. The small town they call home is not far from Stefanie's childhood roots and an easy place to be a writer without all of the business found in the cities to the north and south.

Stefanie is one of those people who, despite quickly approaching middle age, is still trying to decide what to do when she grows up. She has worked in a variety of fields which has given her some great knowledge to work into future books. Now she is trying her hand at writing which she finds quite fulfilling. Stefanie has other works started and is anxious to introduce them to the world in the near future. To follow Stefanie like her Facebook page... or send her an email at stefaniemikota@gmail.com. You can also visit her website at stefaniebridges-mikota.wixsite.com/website.

In His Time

Stefanie Bridges-Mikota